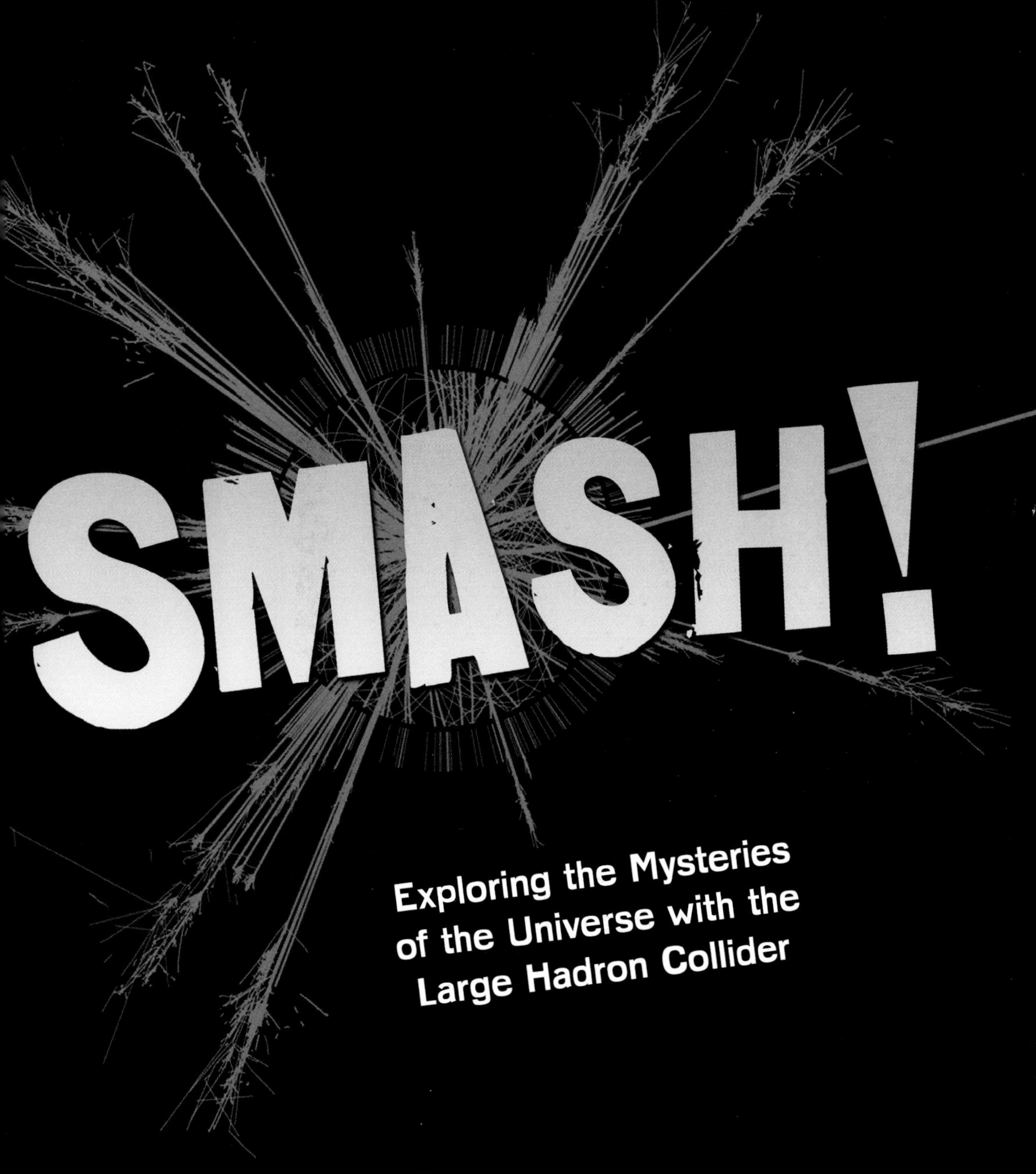

SMASH!

Exploring the Mysteries of the Universe with the Large Hadron Collider

They say an author's books are like her children, and so I dedicate this baby to my husband, Tony Liss, who made it possible. (Alison, Caitlin, and Eli, you're still my favorites!) —S.L.

For Sid and Lena—two charmed quarks —J.W.

Text copyright © 2017 by Sara Latta
Illustrations copyright © 2017 by Jeff Weigel

Graphic Universe™ is a trademark of Lerner Publishing Group, Inc.

Graphic Universe™
A division of Lerner Publishing Group, Inc.
241 First Avenue North
Minneapolis, MN 55401 USA

For reading levels and more information, look up this title at www.lernerbooks.com.

The illustrator has used images from the CERN press office as the basis for some of the artwork for this book.

Main body text set in CCMildMannered 7/8.4.
Typeface provided by Comicraft.

Library of Congress Cataloging-in-Publication Data

Names: Latta, Sara L., author. | Weigel, Jeff, 1958– illustrator.
Title: Smash! : exploring the mysteries of the universe with the Large Hadron Collider / written by Sara Latta ; illustrated by Jeff Weigel.
Other titles: Exploring the mysteries of the universe with the Large Hadron Collider
Description: Minneapolis, MN : Graphic Universe, a division of Lerner Publishing Group, Inc., [2017] | Includes bibliographical references. | Audience: 13–18. | Audience: 9 to 12.
Identifiers: LCCN 2016017321 (print) | LCCN 2016021130 (ebook) | ISBN 9781467785518 (lb ; alk. paper) | ISBN 9781512430707 (pb ; alk. paper) | ISBN 9781512427011 (eb pdf)
Subjects: LCSH: Large Hadron Collider (France and Switzerland)—Juvenile literature. | Higgs bosons—Juvenile literature. | Particles (Nuclear physics)—Juvenile literature. | European Organization for Nuclear Research—Juvenile literature.
Classification: LCC QC787.P73 L38 2017 (print) | LCC QC787.P73 (ebook) | DDC 539.7/36—dc23

LC record available at https://lccn.loc.gov/2016017321

Manufactured in the United States of America
1-37905-19175-7/19/2016

SMASH!

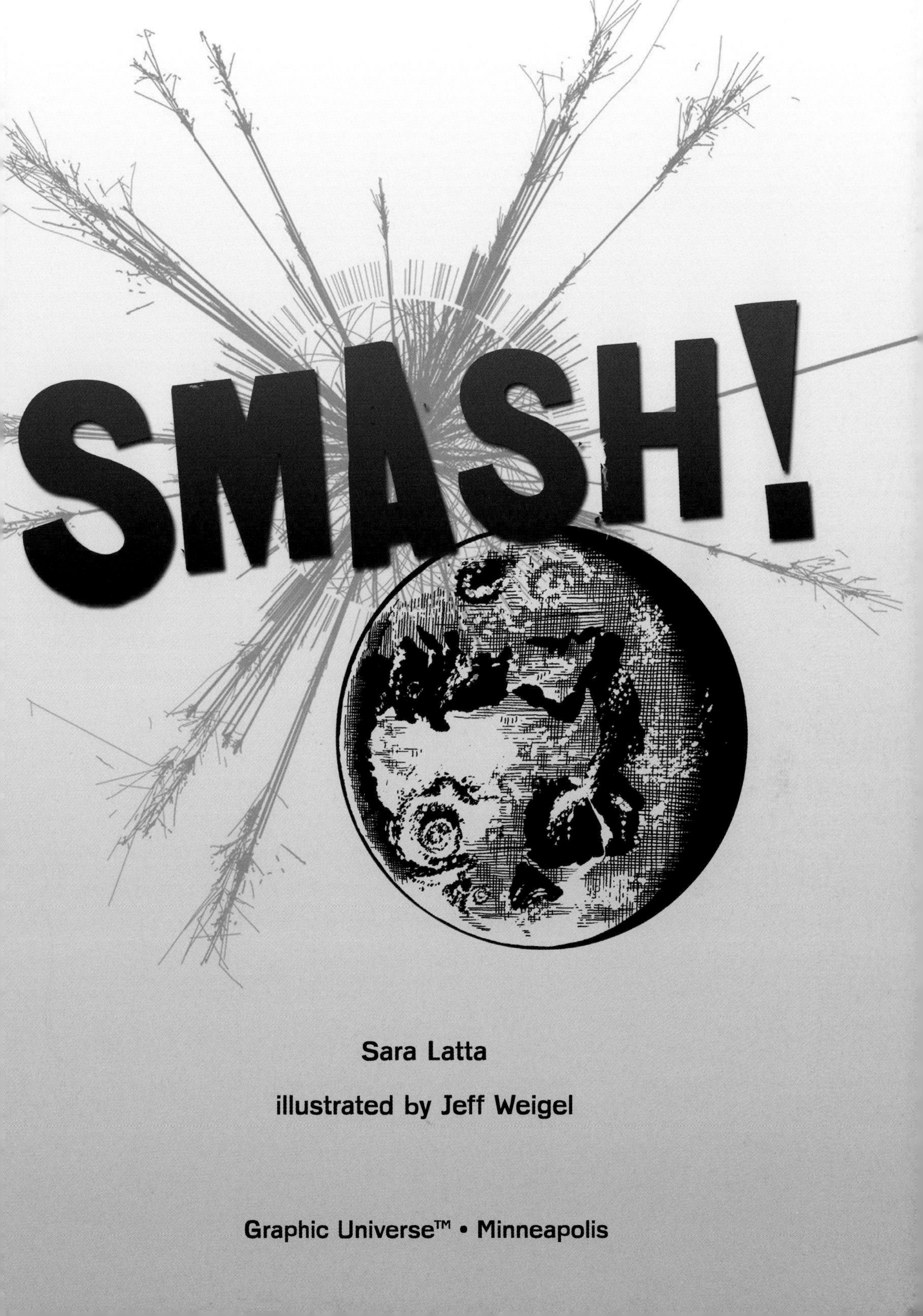

Sara Latta

illustrated by Jeff Weigel

Graphic Universe™ • Minneapolis

Foreword

When I was very little, I spent a lot of time pondering the universe and wondering if it could end—and what that could possibly even mean! I also wondered a lot about "empty" space. I felt certain that if I could take away everything from the space in front of me, including light, what would be left could not be *nothing* . . . but I had no idea what it *could* be. By a very circuitous route, I discovered that physicists are the people who try to answer these questions. This led me to embark on my own study of physics, where I eventually learned to make and use devices for particle accelerators that could detect what actually exists in what we physicists call the "vacuum of space-time."

I am now a professor of physics, and I've spent about thirty-five years searching for and studying fundamental particles with teams of exceptional physicists, engineers, students and technicians on a number of great experiments. We've made some magnificent discoveries, all of which are included in *Smash!*.

There is no doubt now that the vacuum of space-time is not empty. It is filled with the Higgs field, verified by the discovery of the Higgs boson. (You'll learn more about all of this in the pages that follow.) On July 4, 2012, Fabiola Gianotti and I—the leaders of the CERN facility's ATLAS and CMS experiments at the time—announced this discovery. Though a confirmation of the Higgs boson completes a theory of nature at its most fundamental level, it is not the end of the story by any means. This theory, the Standard Model, only represents what we understand—and that is less than 5 percent of the universe.

Sara Latta and Jeff Weigel's graphic novel gives a nicely illustrated and humorous view of the study of particle physics at CERN, the laboratory where the Higgs was discovered. Latta does a marvelous job of encapsulating the incredible history of physical thought, from the pre-Socratic Greek philosophers to modern-day particle physicists at the Large Hadron Collider. It's very accessible, entertaining, and thorough. It covers pretty much everything we know!

Smash! presents all of the fundamental particles and forces, which I like to call "the genetic code of our universe," to the non-expert in a way that may be the best I have seen to date. Weigel's illustrations depict the interactions of quarks, leptons, and force-carrying bosons in a way that's easy to remember. And then, like a Hollywood teaser for a sequel, the graphic novel ends with a glimpse of our current focus on what lies beyond the Standard Model, in the dark side of the universe. I don't think very many people know we've entered these completely uncharted new territories.

Smash! does a great job of showing how the discovery of the Higgs boson marks the end of one era and the beginning of a new one. I believe that *Smash!* will inspire kids who ponder the universe and its vast emptiness, like I did years ago, to join us in this millennia-old quest to understand where we are and how it all works.

Joe Incandela
Yzurdiaga Chair in Experimental Science and Distinguished Professor of Physics
University of California Santa Barbara
Member, National Academy of Sciences

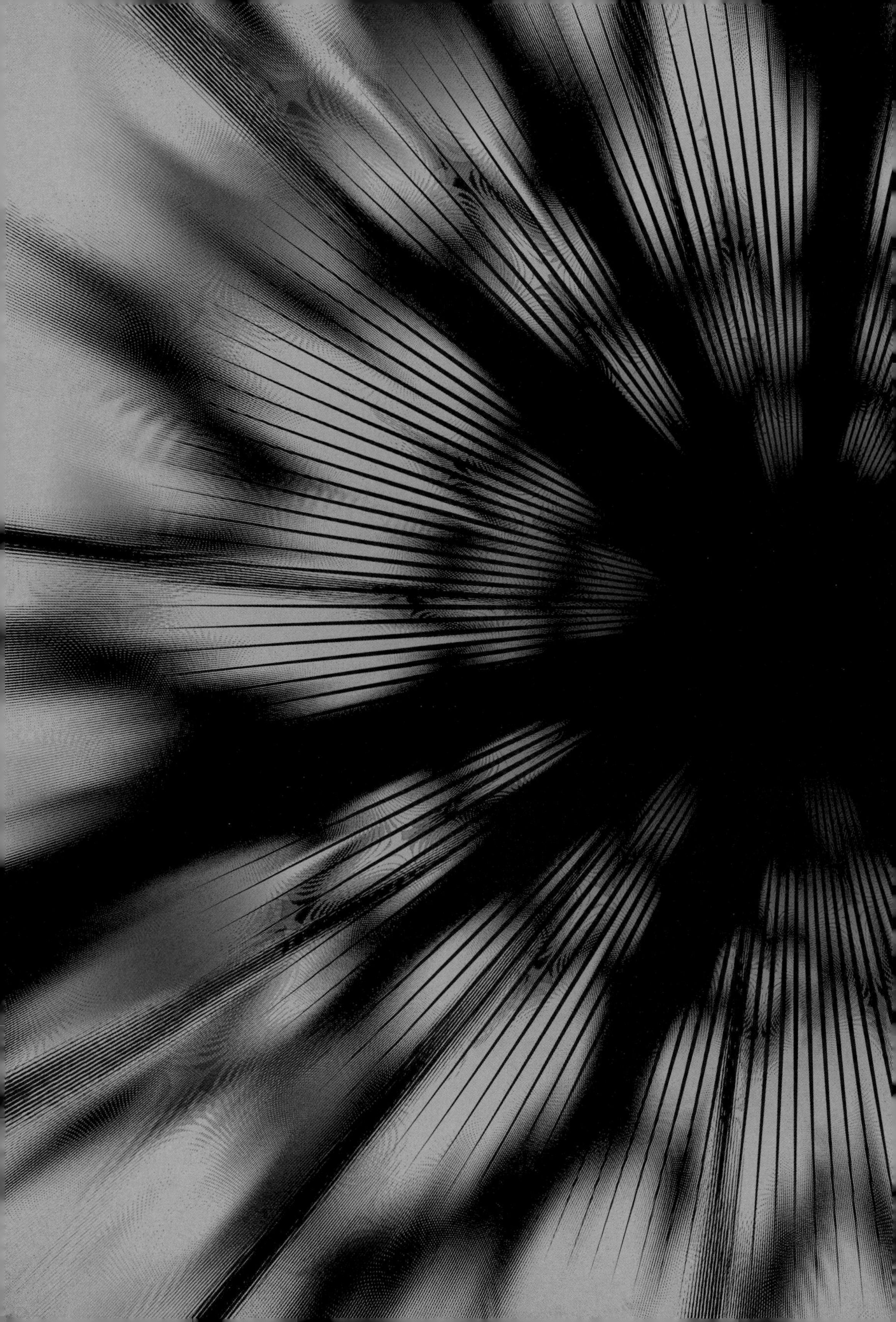

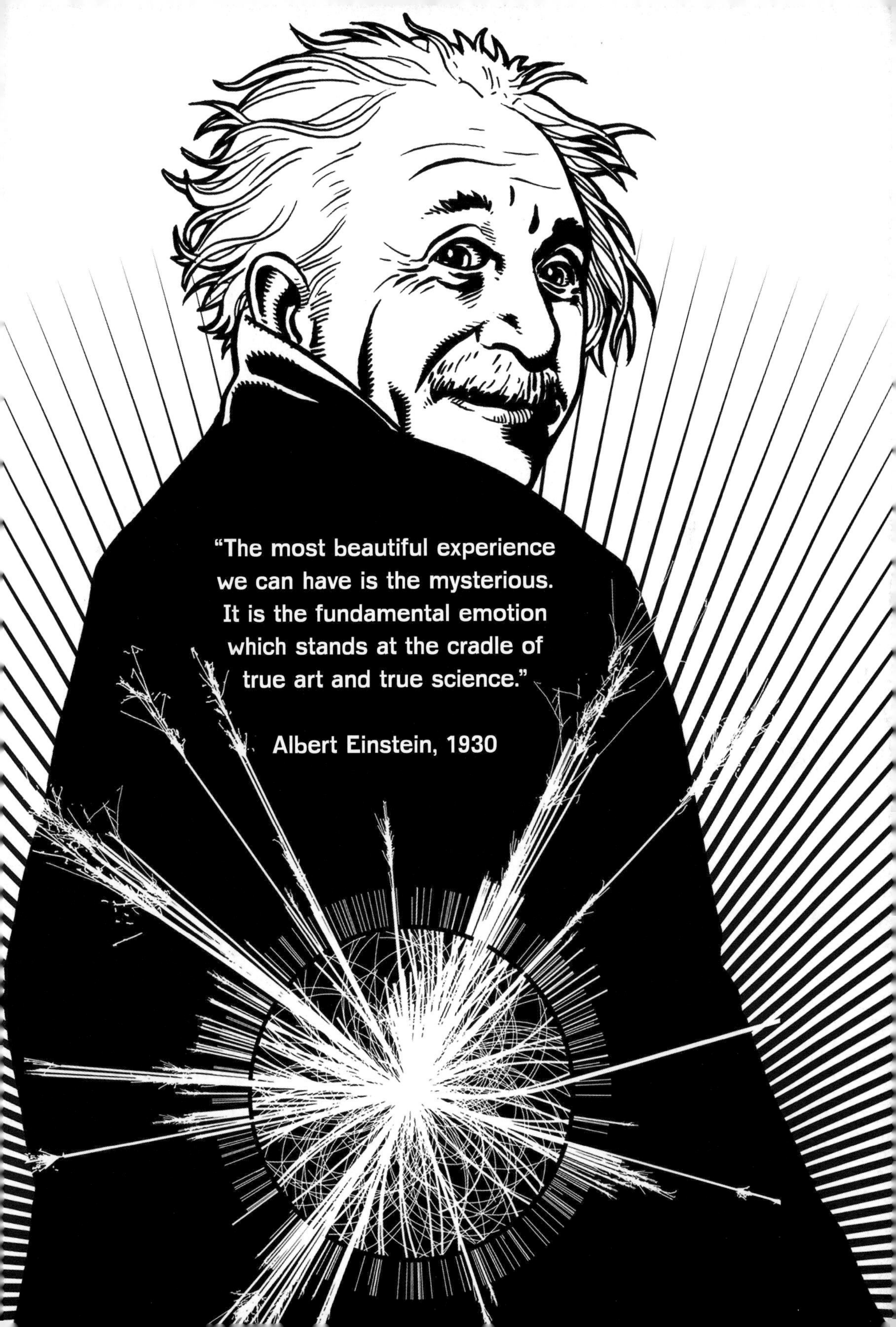
"The most beautiful experience we can have is the mysterious. It is the fundamental emotion which stands at the cradle of true art and true science."
Albert Einstein, 1930

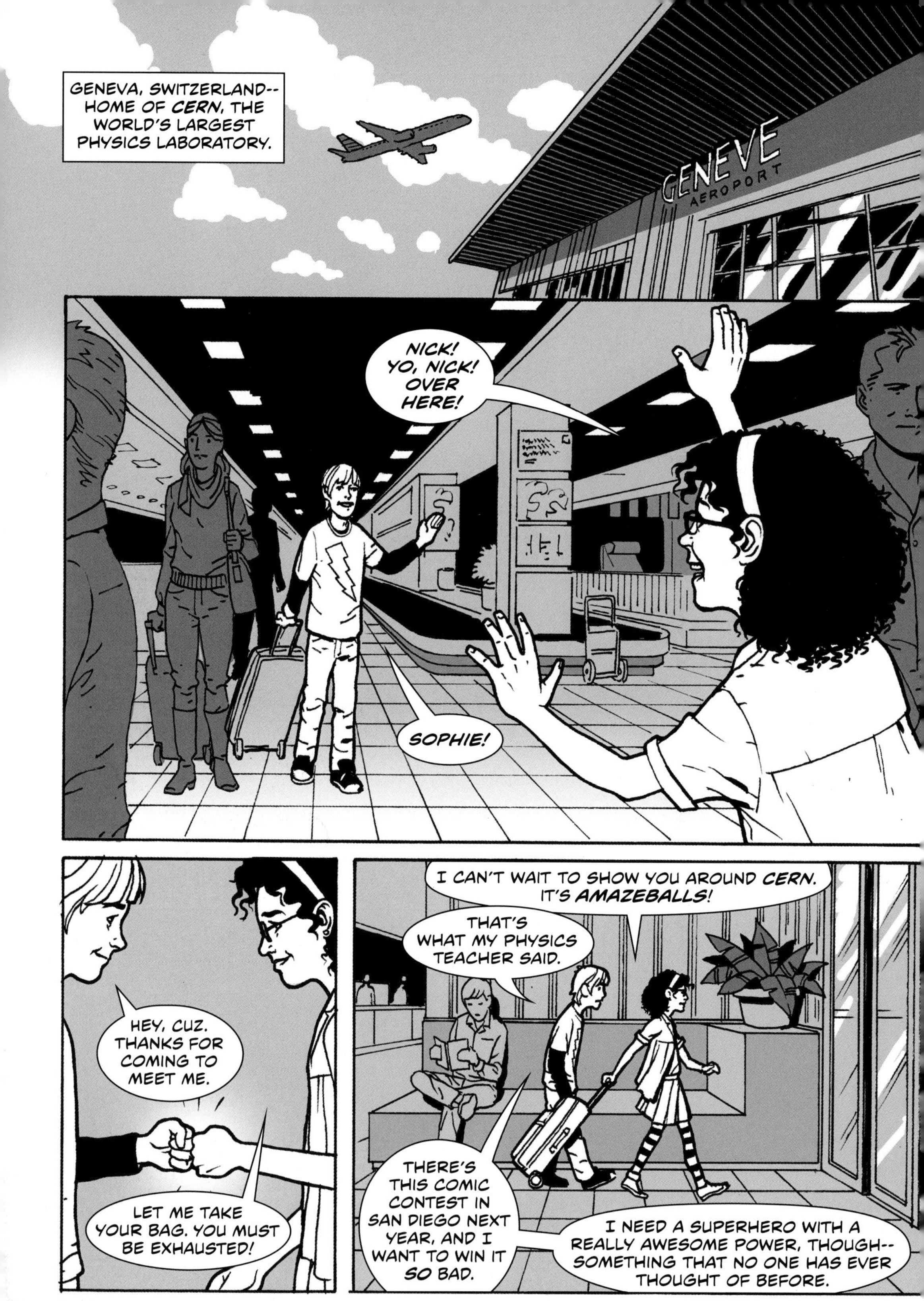
GENEVA, SWITZERLAND--HOME OF CERN, THE WORLD'S LARGEST PHYSICS LABORATORY.
GENEVE AEROPORT
NICK! YO, NICK! OVER HERE!
SOPHIE!
HEY, CUZ. THANKS FOR COMING TO MEET ME.
LET ME TAKE YOUR BAG. YOU MUST BE EXHAUSTED!
I CAN'T WAIT TO SHOW YOU AROUND CERN. IT'S AMAZEBALLS!
THAT'S WHAT MY PHYSICS TEACHER SAID.
THERE'S THIS COMIC CONTEST IN SAN DIEGO NEXT YEAR, AND I WANT TO WIN IT SO BAD.
I NEED A SUPERHERO WITH A REALLY AWESOME POWER, THOUGH--SOMETHING THAT NO ONE HAS EVER THOUGHT OF BEFORE.

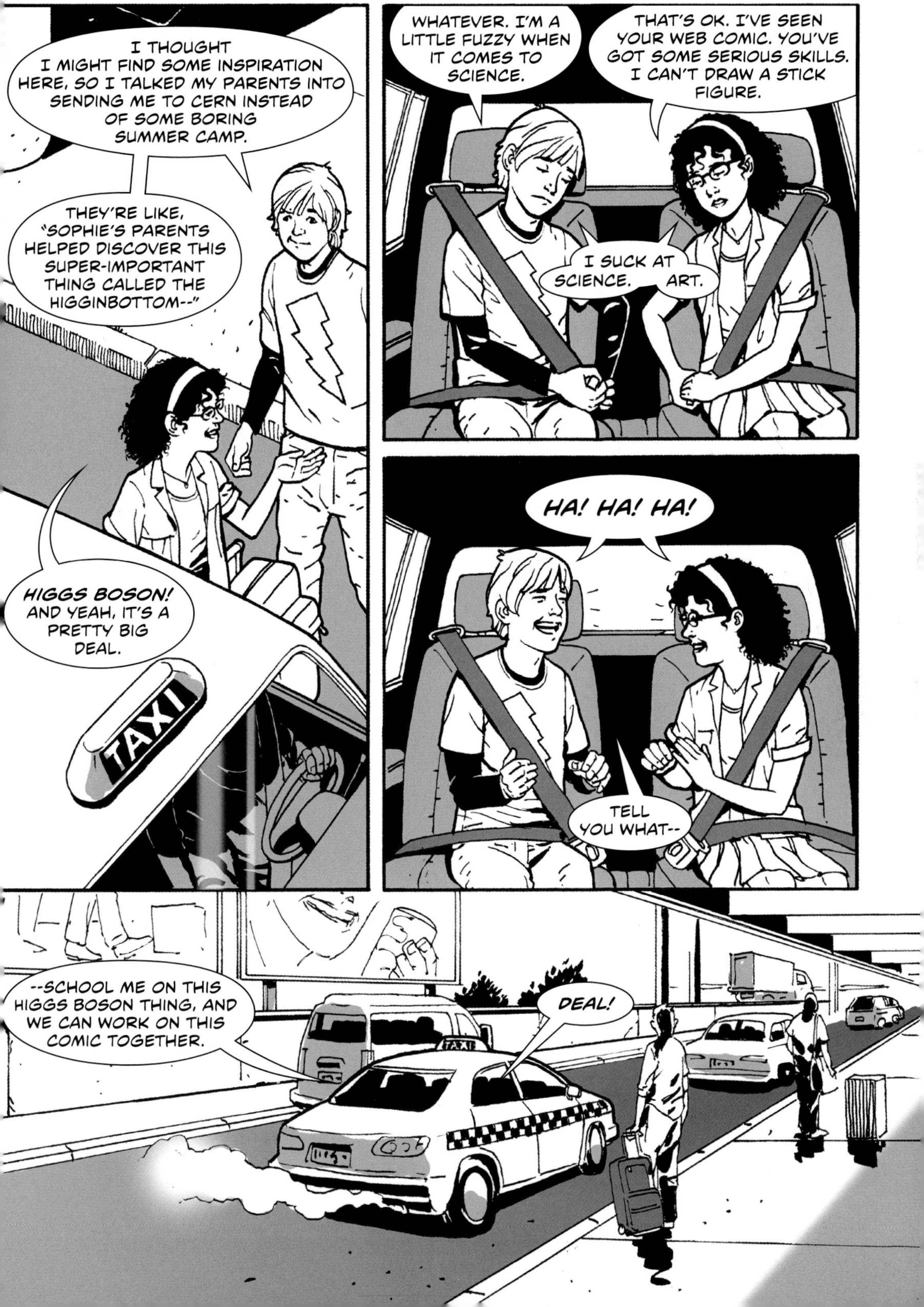
I THOUGHT I MIGHT FIND SOME INSPIRATION HERE, SO I TALKED MY PARENTS INTO SENDING ME TO CERN INSTEAD OF SOME BORING SUMMER CAMP.
THEY'RE LIKE, "SOPHIE'S PARENTS HELPED DISCOVER THIS SUPER-IMPORTANT THING CALLED THE HIGGINBOTTOM--"
HIGGS BOSON! AND YEAH, IT'S A PRETTY BIG DEAL.
TAXI
WHATEVER. I'M A LITTLE FUZZY WHEN IT COMES TO SCIENCE.
THAT'S OK. I'VE SEEN YOUR WEB COMIC. YOU'VE GOT SOME SERIOUS SKILLS. I CAN'T DRAW A STICK FIGURE.
I SUCK AT SCIENCE.
ART.
HA! HA! HA!
TELL YOU WHAT--
--SCHOOL ME ON THIS HIGGS BOSON THING, AND WE CAN WORK ON THIS COMIC TOGETHER.
DEAL!
TAXI

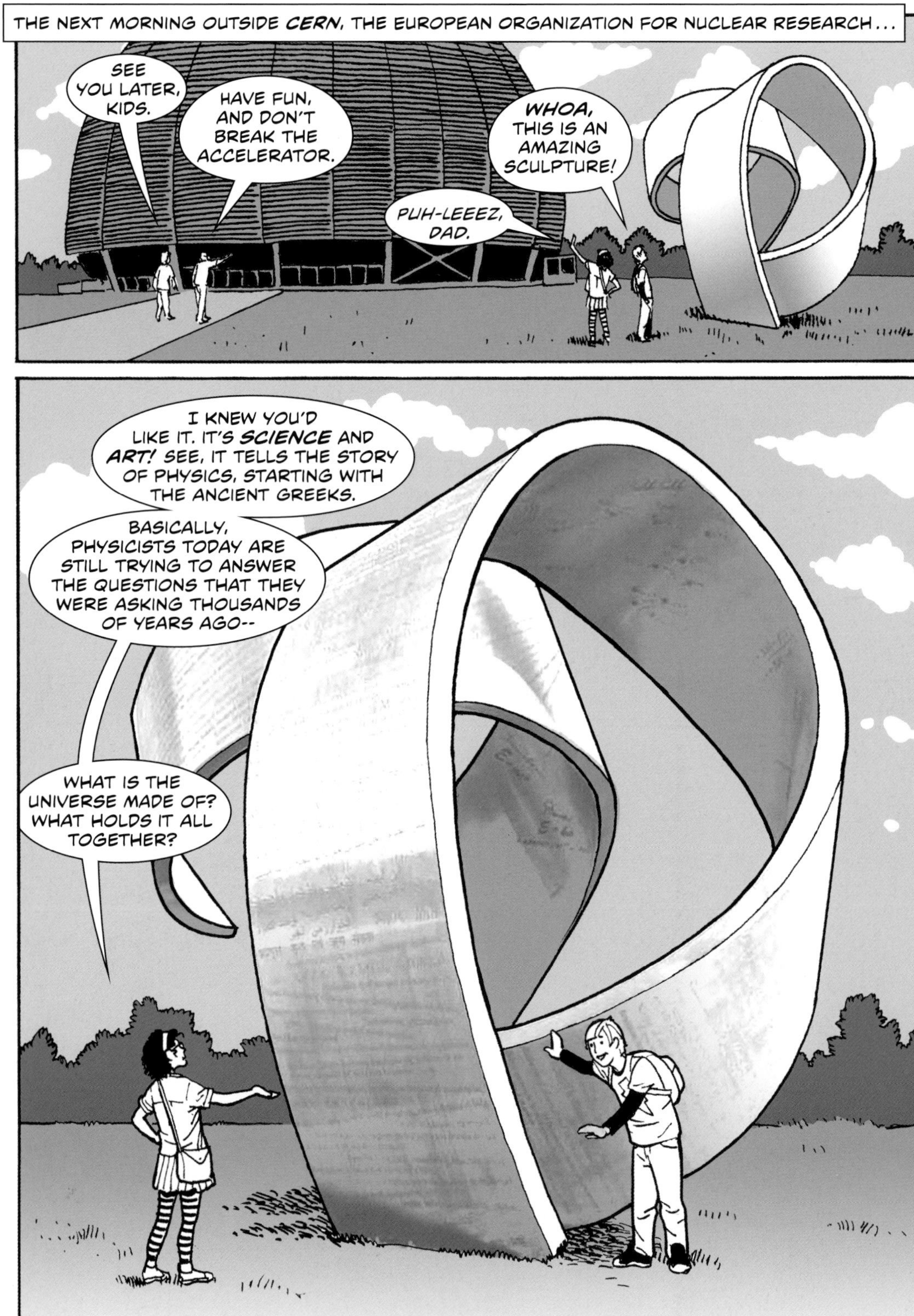
THE NEXT MORNING OUTSIDE CERN, THE EUROPEAN ORGANIZATION FOR NUCLEAR RESEARCH...
SEE YOU LATER, KIDS.
HAVE FUN, AND DON'T BREAK THE ACCELERATOR.
WHOA, THIS IS AN AMAZING SCULPTURE!
PUH-LEEEZ, DAD.
I KNEW YOU'D LIKE IT. IT'S SCIENCE AND ART! SEE, IT TELLS THE STORY OF PHYSICS, STARTING WITH THE ANCIENT GREEKS.
BASICALLY, PHYSICISTS TODAY ARE STILL TRYING TO ANSWER THE QUESTIONS THAT THEY WERE ASKING THOUSANDS OF YEARS AGO--
WHAT IS THE UNIVERSE MADE OF? WHAT HOLDS IT ALL TOGETHER?

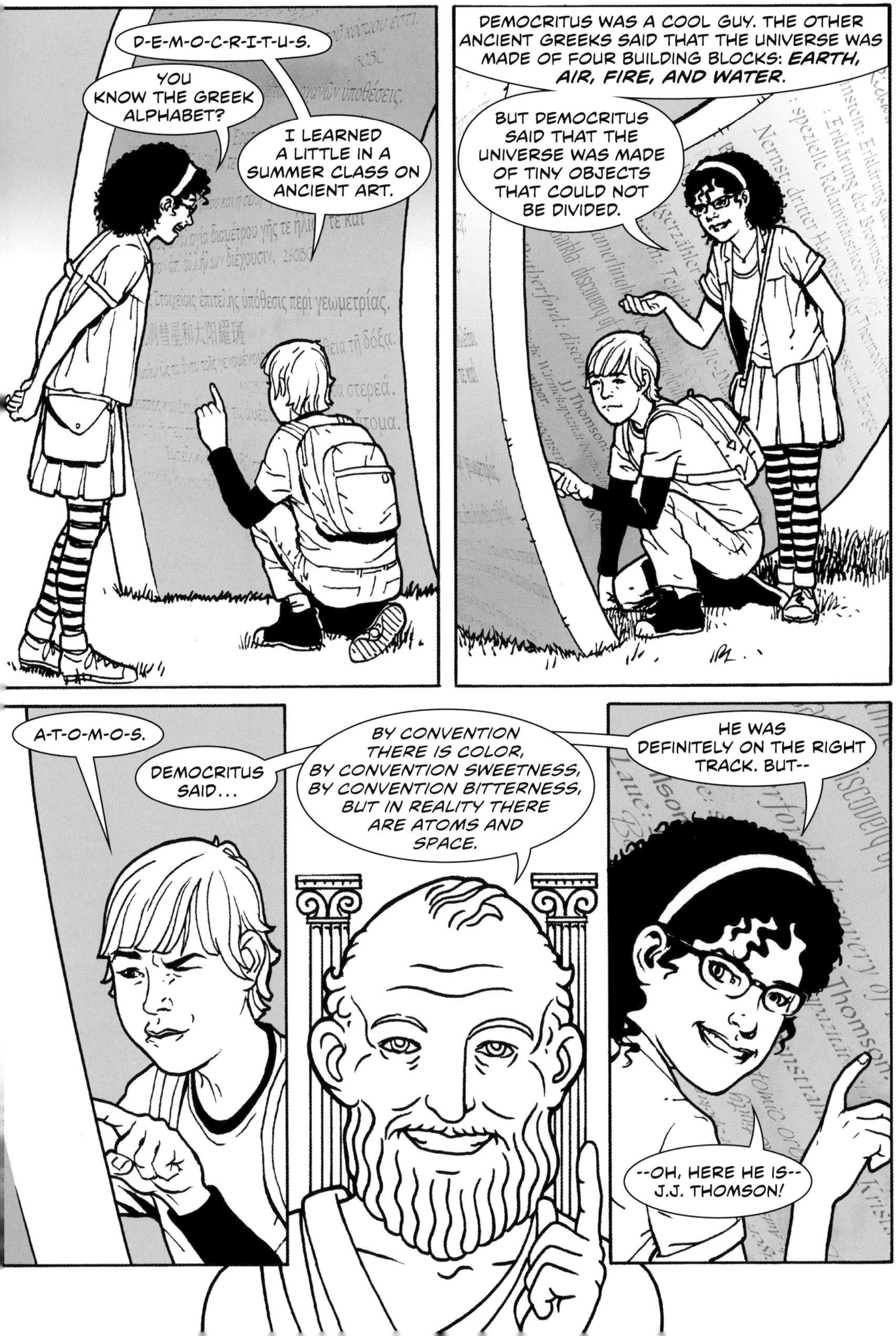
D-E-M-O-C-R-I-T-U-S.
YOU KNOW THE GREEK ALPHABET?
I LEARNED A LITTLE IN A SUMMER CLASS ON ANCIENT ART.
DEMOCRITUS WAS A COOL GUY. THE OTHER ANCIENT GREEKS SAID THAT THE UNIVERSE WAS MADE OF FOUR BUILDING BLOCKS: EARTH, AIR, FIRE, AND WATER.
BUT DEMOCRITUS SAID THAT THE UNIVERSE WAS MADE OF TINY OBJECTS THAT COULD NOT BE DIVIDED.
A-T-O-M-O-S.
DEMOCRITUS SAID...
BY CONVENTION THERE IS COLOR, BY CONVENTION SWEETNESS, BY CONVENTION BITTERNESS, BUT IN REALITY THERE ARE ATOMS AND SPACE.
HE WAS DEFINITELY ON THE RIGHT TRACK. BUT--
--OH, HERE HE IS-- J.J. THOMSON!

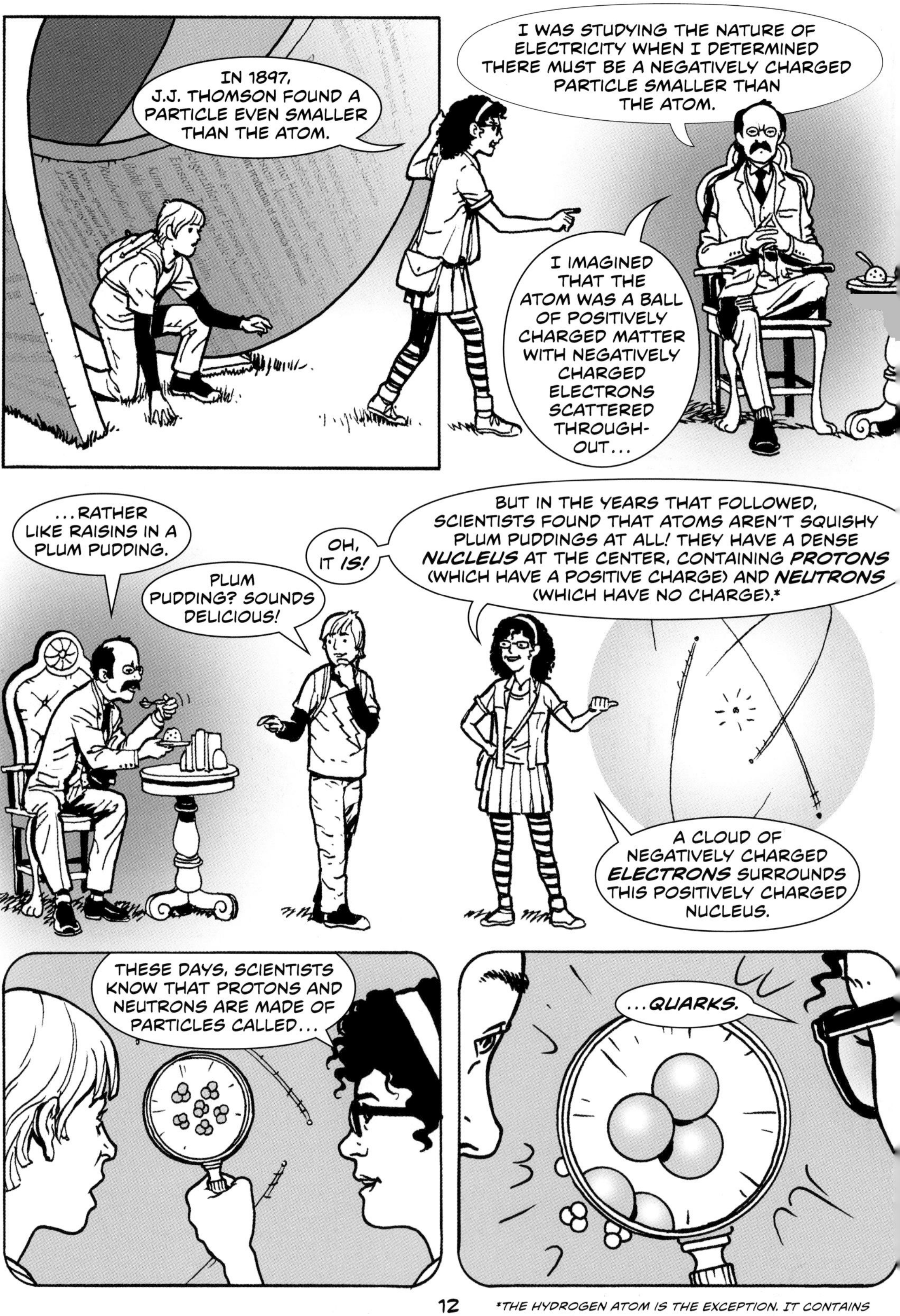
IN 1897, J.J. THOMSON FOUND A PARTICLE EVEN SMALLER THAN THE ATOM.
I WAS STUDYING THE NATURE OF ELECTRICITY WHEN I DETERMINED THERE MUST BE A NEGATIVELY CHARGED PARTICLE SMALLER THAN THE ATOM.
I IMAGINED THAT THE ATOM WAS A BALL OF POSITIVELY CHARGED MATTER WITH NEGATIVELY CHARGED ELECTRONS SCATTERED THROUGH- OUT...
...RATHER LIKE RAISINS IN A PLUM PUDDING.
PLUM PUDDING? SOUNDS DELICIOUS!
OH, IT *IS!*
BUT IN THE YEARS THAT FOLLOWED, SCIENTISTS FOUND THAT ATOMS AREN'T SQUISHY PLUM PUDDINGS AT ALL! THEY HAVE A DENSE ***NUCLEUS*** AT THE CENTER, CONTAINING ***PROTONS*** (WHICH HAVE A POSITIVE CHARGE) AND ***NEUTRONS*** (WHICH HAVE NO CHARGE).*
A CLOUD OF NEGATIVELY CHARGED ***ELECTRONS*** SURROUNDS THIS POSITIVELY CHARGED NUCLEUS.
THESE DAYS, SCIENTISTS KNOW THAT PROTONS AND NEUTRONS ARE MADE OF PARTICLES CALLED...
...***QUARKS.***

**THE HYDROGEN ATOM IS THE EXCEPTION. IT CONTAINS JUST ONE PROTON AND ONE ELECTRON.*

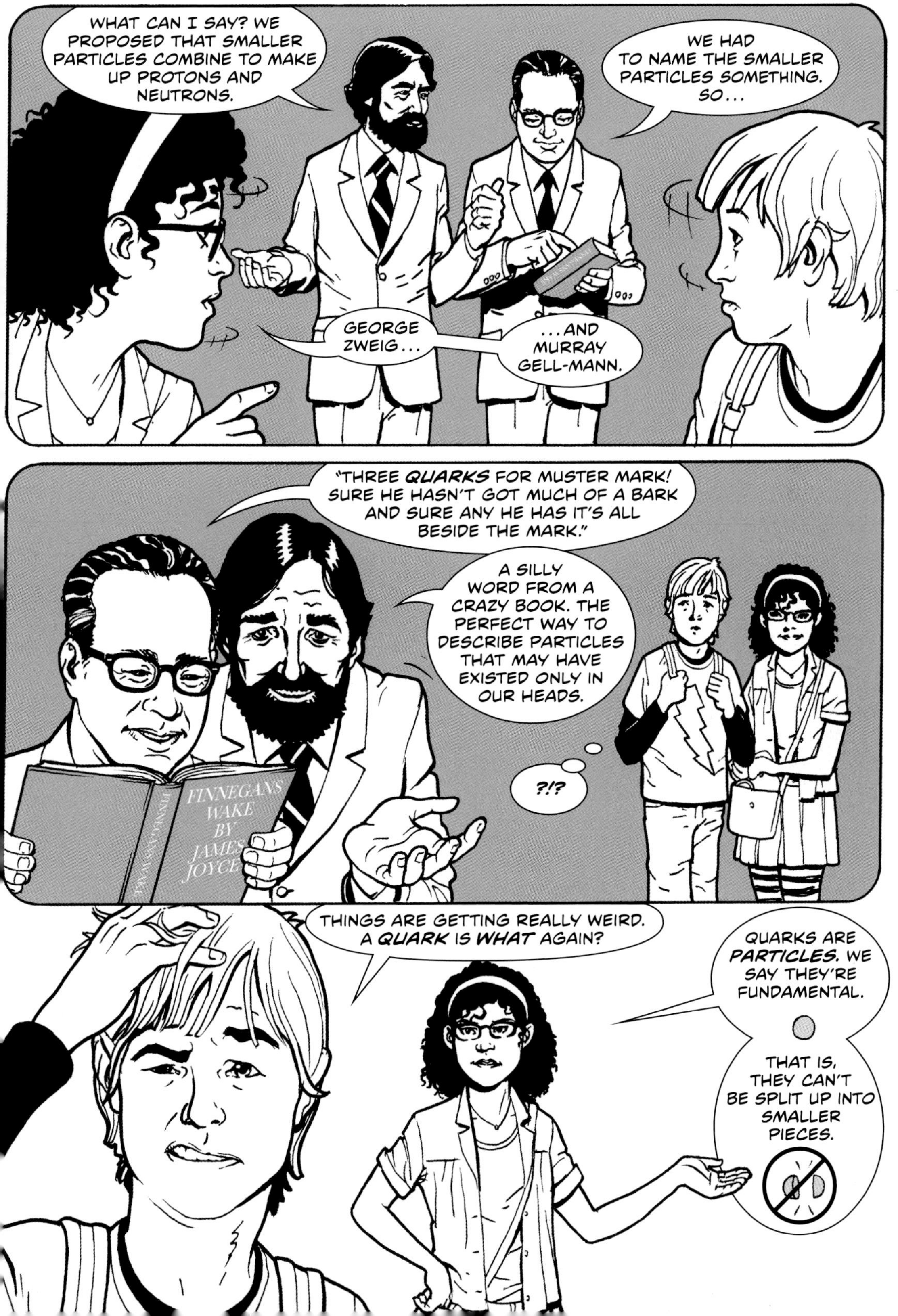
WHAT CAN I SAY? WE PROPOSED THAT SMALLER PARTICLES COMBINE TO MAKE UP PROTONS AND NEUTRONS.
WE HAD TO NAME THE SMALLER PARTICLES SOMETHING. SO...
GEORGE ZWEIG...
...AND MURRAY GELL-MANN.
"THREE QUARKS FOR MUSTER MARK! SURE HE HASN'T GOT MUCH OF A BARK AND SURE ANY HE HAS IT'S ALL BESIDE THE MARK."
A SILLY WORD FROM A CRAZY BOOK. THE PERFECT WAY TO DESCRIBE PARTICLES THAT MAY HAVE EXISTED ONLY IN OUR HEADS.
FINNEGANS WAKE BY JAMES JOYCE
?!?
THINGS ARE GETTING REALLY WEIRD. A QUARK IS WHAT AGAIN?
QUARKS ARE PARTICLES. WE SAY THEY'RE FUNDAMENTAL.
THAT IS, THEY CAN'T BE SPLIT UP INTO SMALLER PIECES.

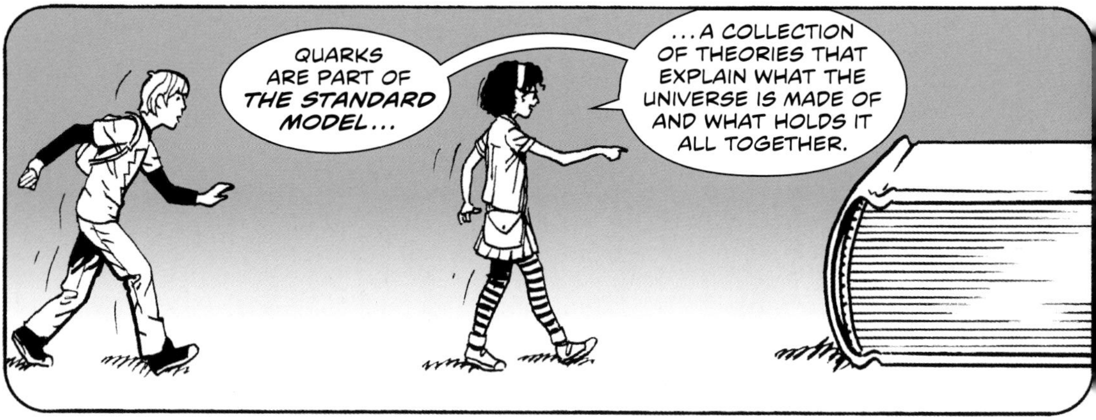
QUARKS ARE PART OF *THE STANDARD MODEL...*
...A COLLECTION OF THEORIES THAT EXPLAIN WHAT THE UNIVERSE IS MADE OF AND WHAT HOLDS IT ALL TOGETHER.

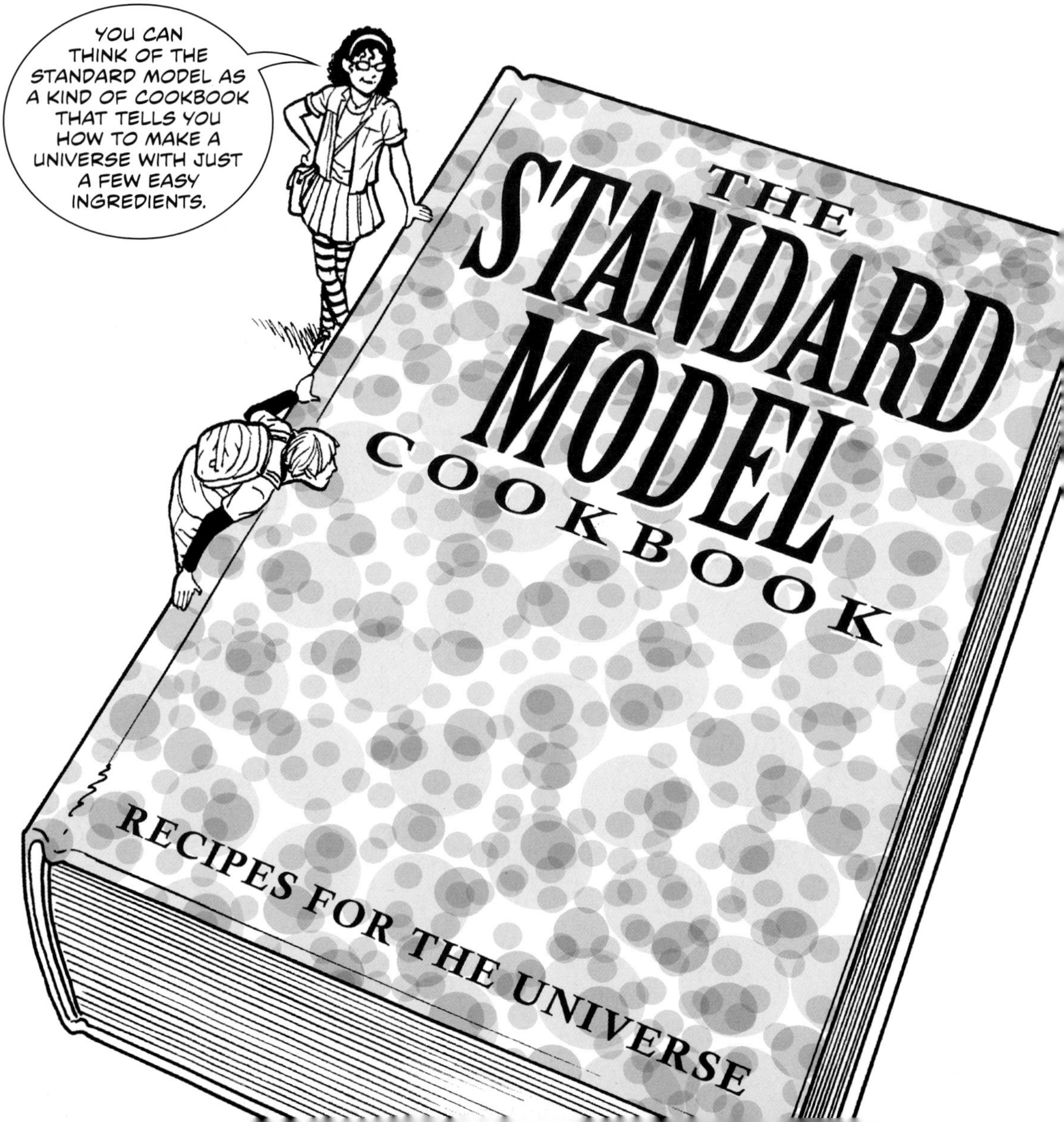
YOU CAN THINK OF THE STANDARD MODEL AS A KIND OF COOKBOOK THAT TELLS YOU HOW TO MAKE A UNIVERSE WITH JUST A FEW EASY INGREDIENTS.
THE STANDARD MODEL COOKBOOK
RECIPES FOR THE UNIVERSE

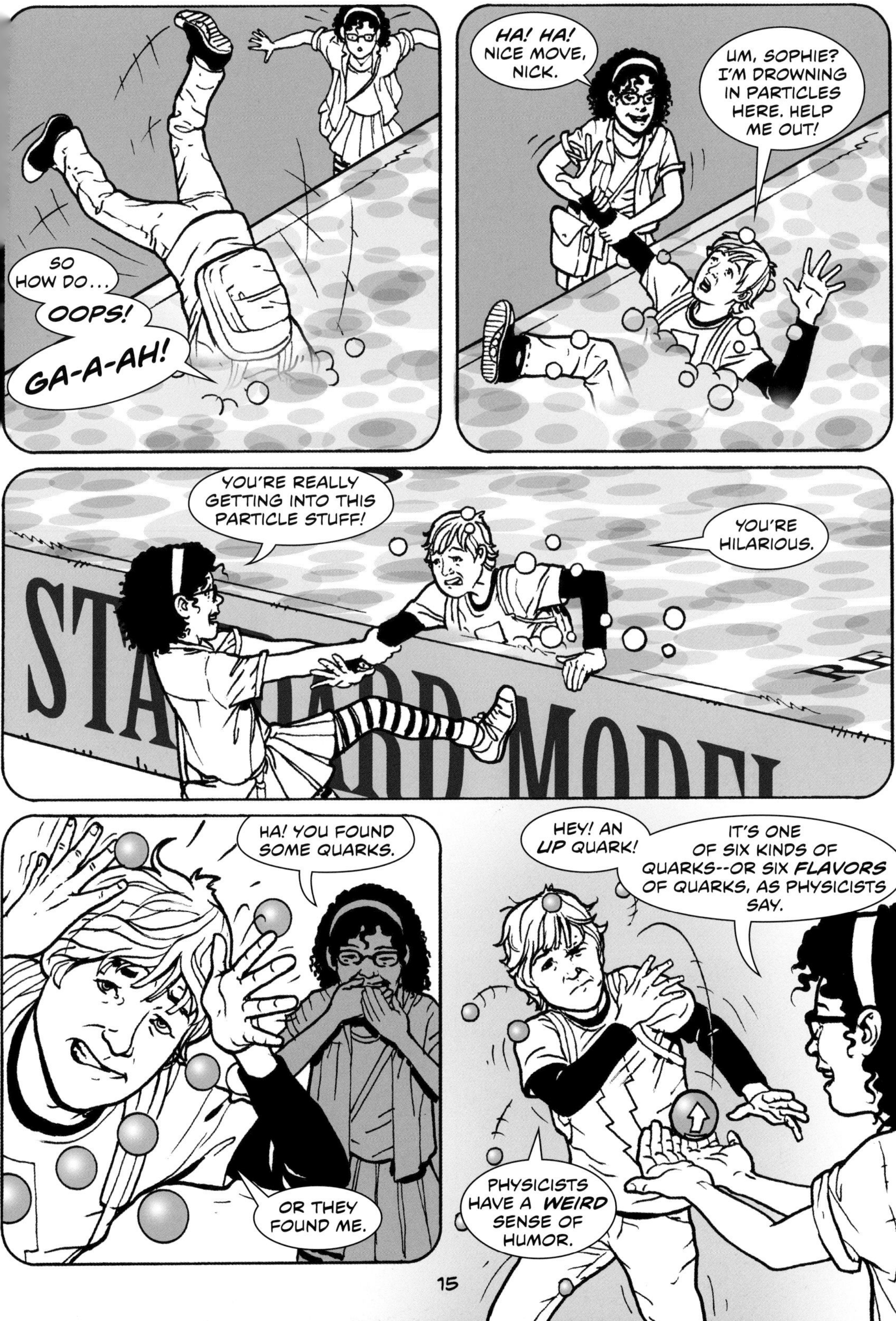
SO HOW DO...
OOPS!
GA-A-AH!
HA! HA! NICE MOVE, NICK.
UM, SOPHIE? I'M DROWNING IN PARTICLES HERE. HELP ME OUT!
YOU'RE REALLY GETTING INTO THIS PARTICLE STUFF!
YOU'RE HILARIOUS.
STANDARD MODEL
HA! YOU FOUND SOME QUARKS.
OR THEY FOUND ME.
HEY! AN *UP* QUARK!
IT'S ONE OF SIX KINDS OF QUARKS--OR SIX *FLAVORS* OF QUARKS, AS PHYSICISTS SAY.
PHYSICISTS HAVE A *WEIRD* SENSE OF HUMOR.

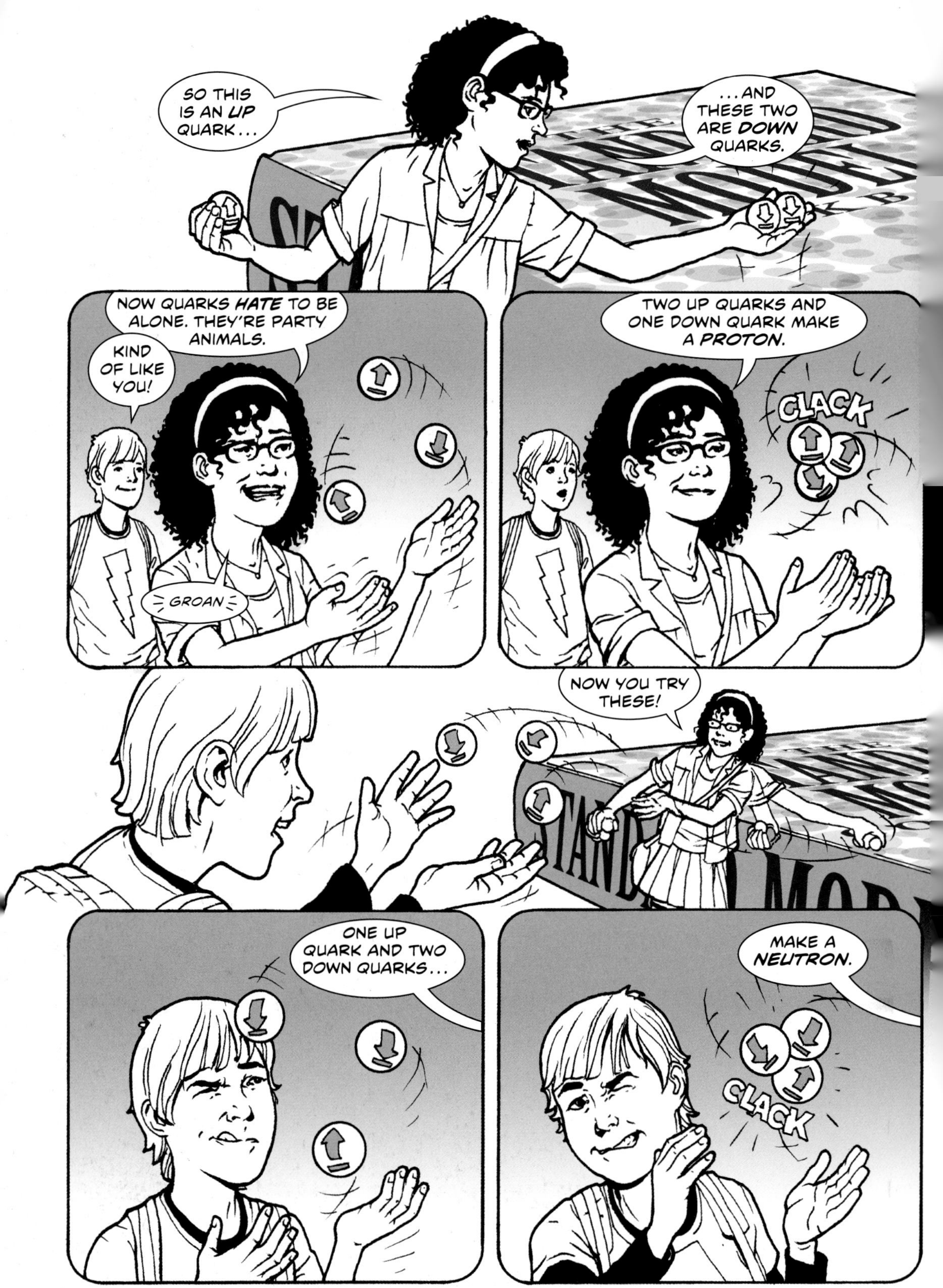
SO THIS IS AN *UP* QUARK...
...AND THESE TWO ARE *DOWN* QUARKS.
NOW QUARKS *HATE* TO BE ALONE. THEY'RE PARTY ANIMALS.
KIND OF LIKE YOU!
GROAN
TWO UP QUARKS AND ONE DOWN QUARK MAKE A *PROTON*.
CLACK
NOW YOU TRY THESE!
ONE UP QUARK AND TWO DOWN QUARKS...
MAKE A *NEUTRON*.
CLACK

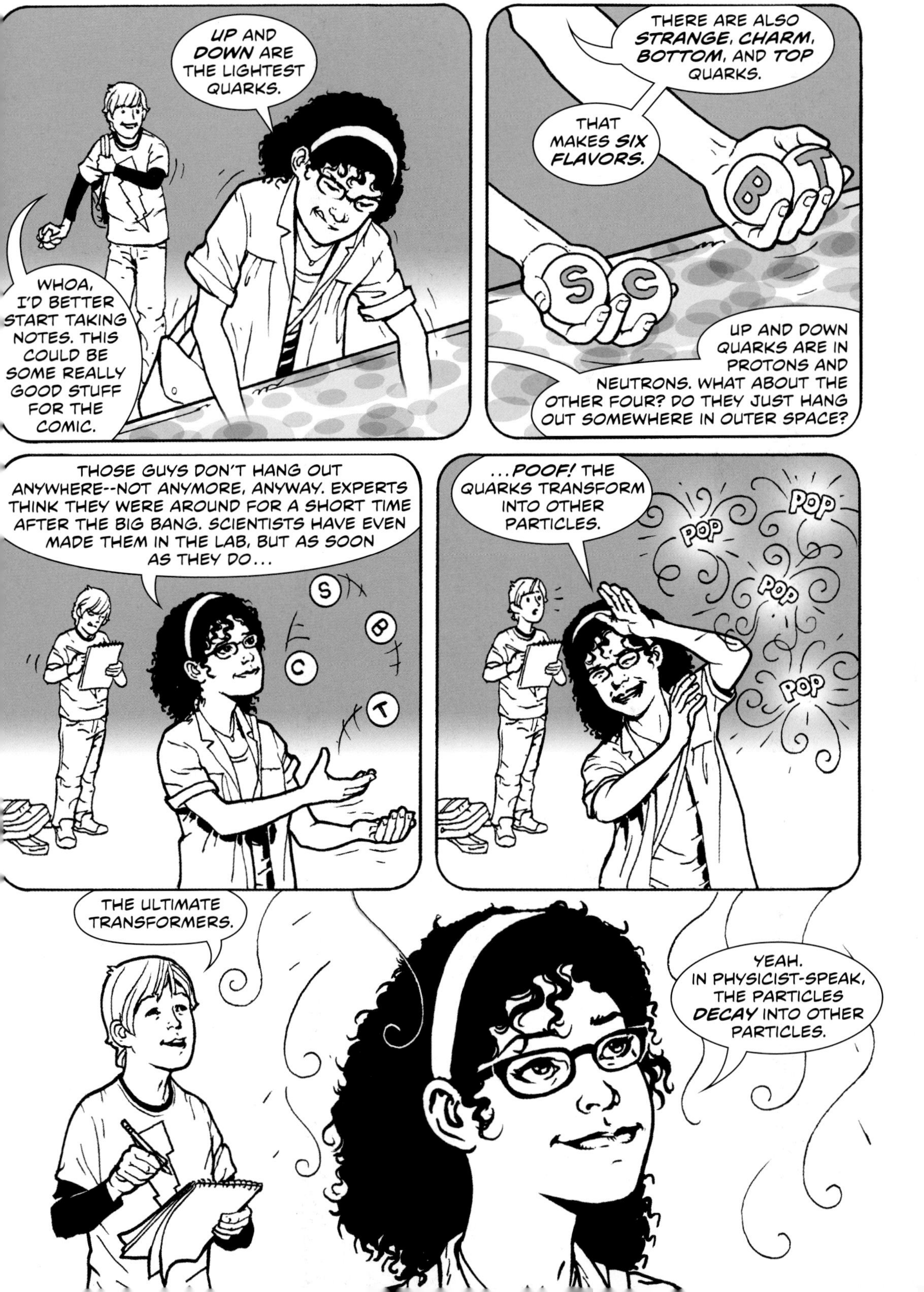
UP AND DOWN ARE THE LIGHTEST QUARKS.
WHOA, I'D BETTER START TAKING NOTES. THIS COULD BE SOME REALLY GOOD STUFF FOR THE COMIC.
THERE ARE ALSO STRANGE, CHARM, BOTTOM, AND TOP QUARKS.
THAT MAKES SIX FLAVORS.
B
T
S
C
UP AND DOWN QUARKS ARE IN PROTONS AND NEUTRONS. WHAT ABOUT THE OTHER FOUR? DO THEY JUST HANG OUT SOMEWHERE IN OUTER SPACE?
THOSE GUYS DON'T HANG OUT ANYWHERE--NOT ANYMORE, ANYWAY. EXPERTS THINK THEY WERE AROUND FOR A SHORT TIME AFTER THE BIG BANG. SCIENTISTS HAVE EVEN MADE THEM IN THE LAB, BUT AS SOON AS THEY DO...
S
B
C
T
...POOF! THE QUARKS TRANSFORM INTO OTHER PARTICLES.
POP
POP
POP
POP
THE ULTIMATE TRANSFORMERS.
YEAH. IN PHYSICIST-SPEAK, THE PARTICLES DECAY INTO OTHER PARTICLES.

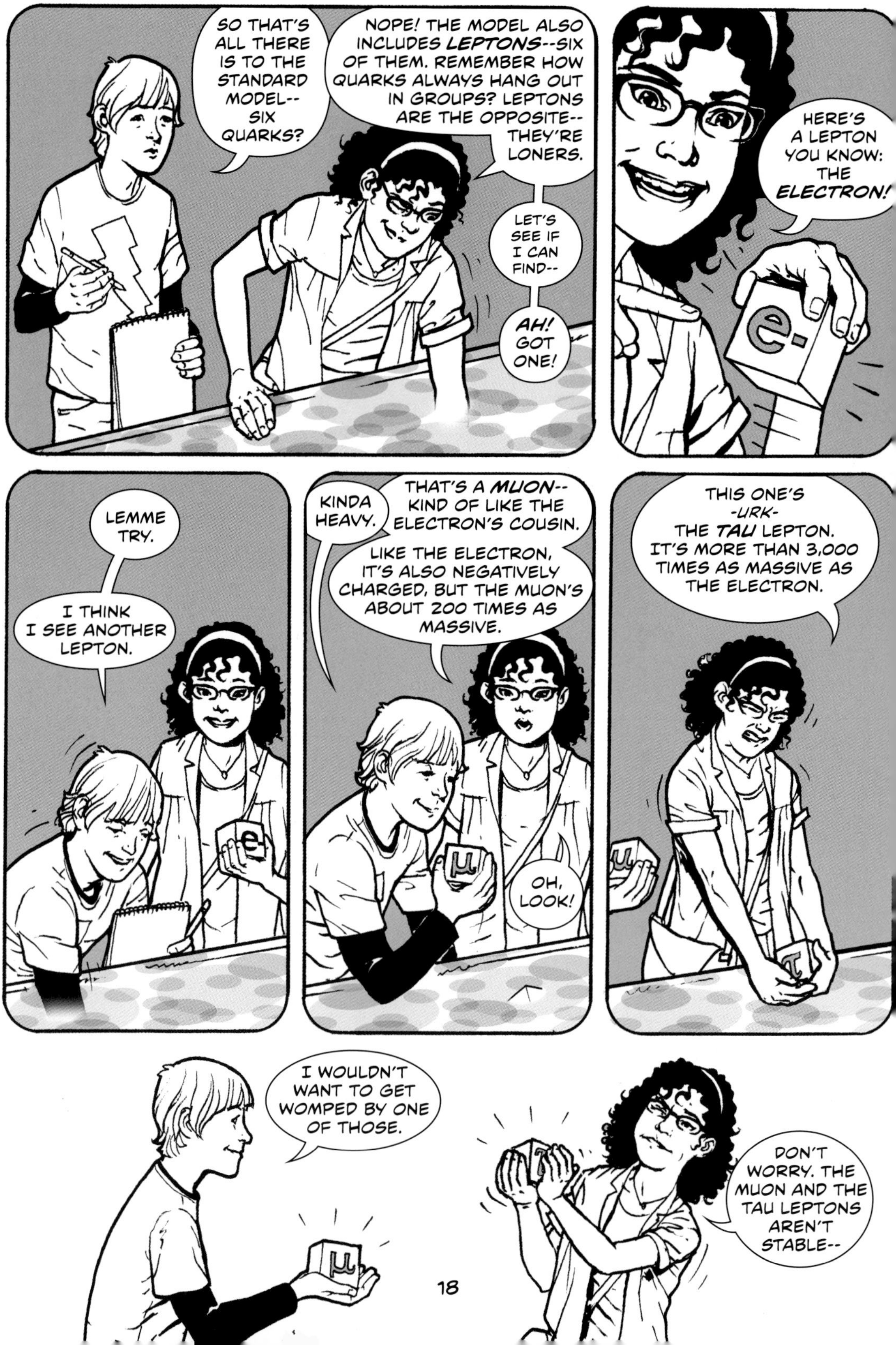
SO THAT'S ALL THERE IS TO THE STANDARD MODEL-- SIX QUARKS?
NOPE! THE MODEL ALSO INCLUDES **LEPTONS**--SIX OF THEM. REMEMBER HOW QUARKS ALWAYS HANG OUT IN GROUPS? LEPTONS ARE THE OPPOSITE-- THEY'RE LONERS.
LET'S SEE IF I CAN FIND--
AH! GOT ONE!
HERE'S A LEPTON YOU KNOW: THE **ELECTRON!**
e-
LEMME TRY.
I THINK I SEE ANOTHER LEPTON.
e
KINDA HEAVY.
THAT'S A **MUON**-- KIND OF LIKE THE ELECTRON'S COUSIN.
LIKE THE ELECTRON, IT'S ALSO NEGATIVELY CHARGED, BUT THE MUON'S ABOUT 200 TIMES AS MASSIVE.
μ
OH, LOOK!
THIS ONE'S *-URK-* THE **TAU** LEPTON. IT'S MORE THAN 3,000 TIMES AS MASSIVE AS THE ELECTRON.
μ
τ
I WOULDN'T WANT TO GET WOMPED BY ONE OF THOSE.
μ
τ
DON'T WORRY. THE MUON AND THE TAU LEPTONS AREN'T STABLE--

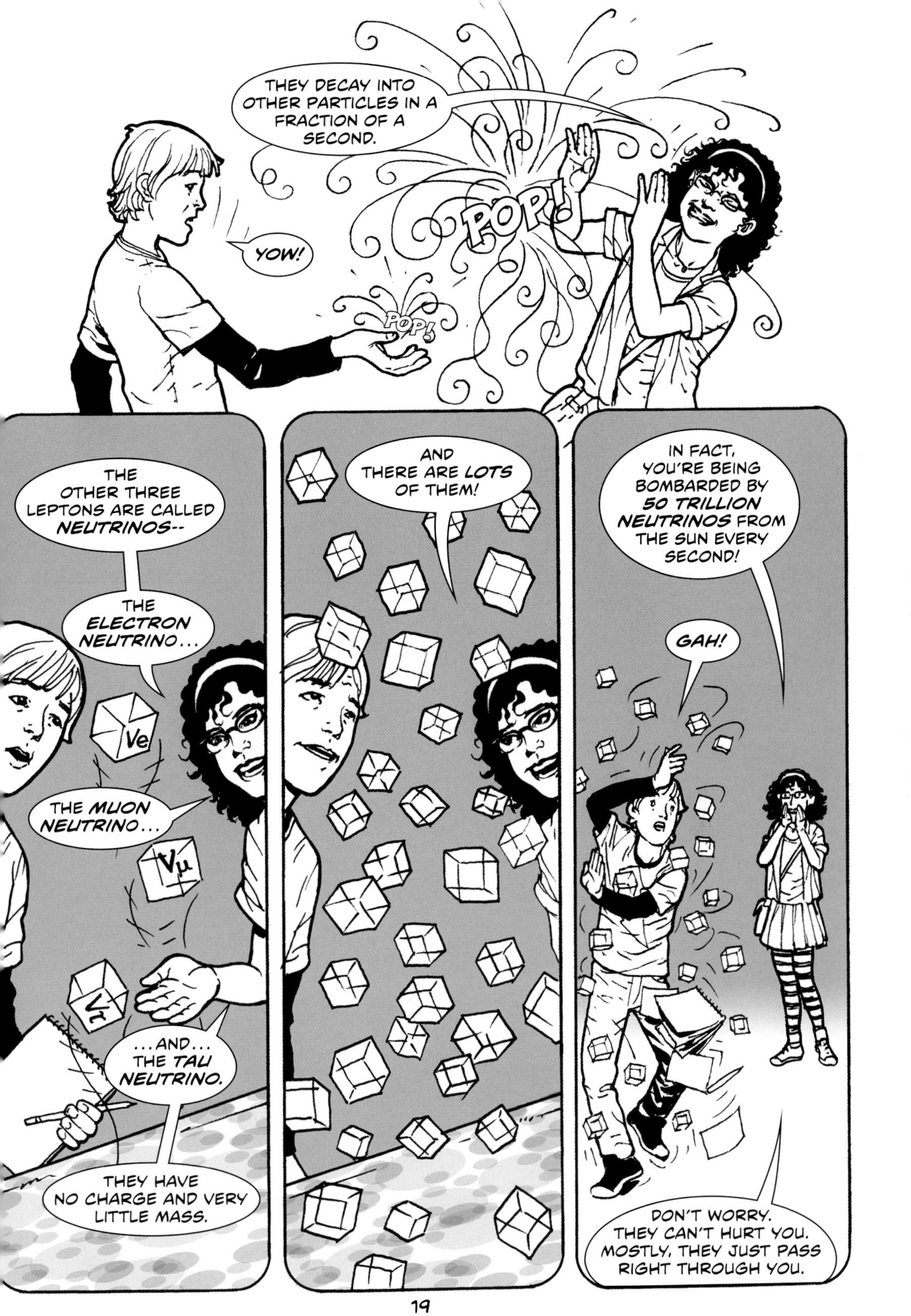
THEY DECAY INTO OTHER PARTICLES IN A FRACTION OF A SECOND.
YOW!
POP!
POP!
THE OTHER THREE LEPTONS ARE CALLED NEUTRINOS--
THE ELECTRON NEUTRINO...
Ve
THE MUON NEUTRINO...
Vμ
Vτ
...AND... THE TAU NEUTRINO.
THEY HAVE NO CHARGE AND VERY LITTLE MASS.
AND THERE ARE LOTS OF THEM!
IN FACT, YOU'RE BEING BOMBARDED BY 50 TRILLION NEUTRINOS FROM THE SUN EVERY SECOND!
GAH!
DON'T WORRY. THEY CAN'T HURT YOU. MOSTLY, THEY JUST PASS RIGHT THROUGH YOU.

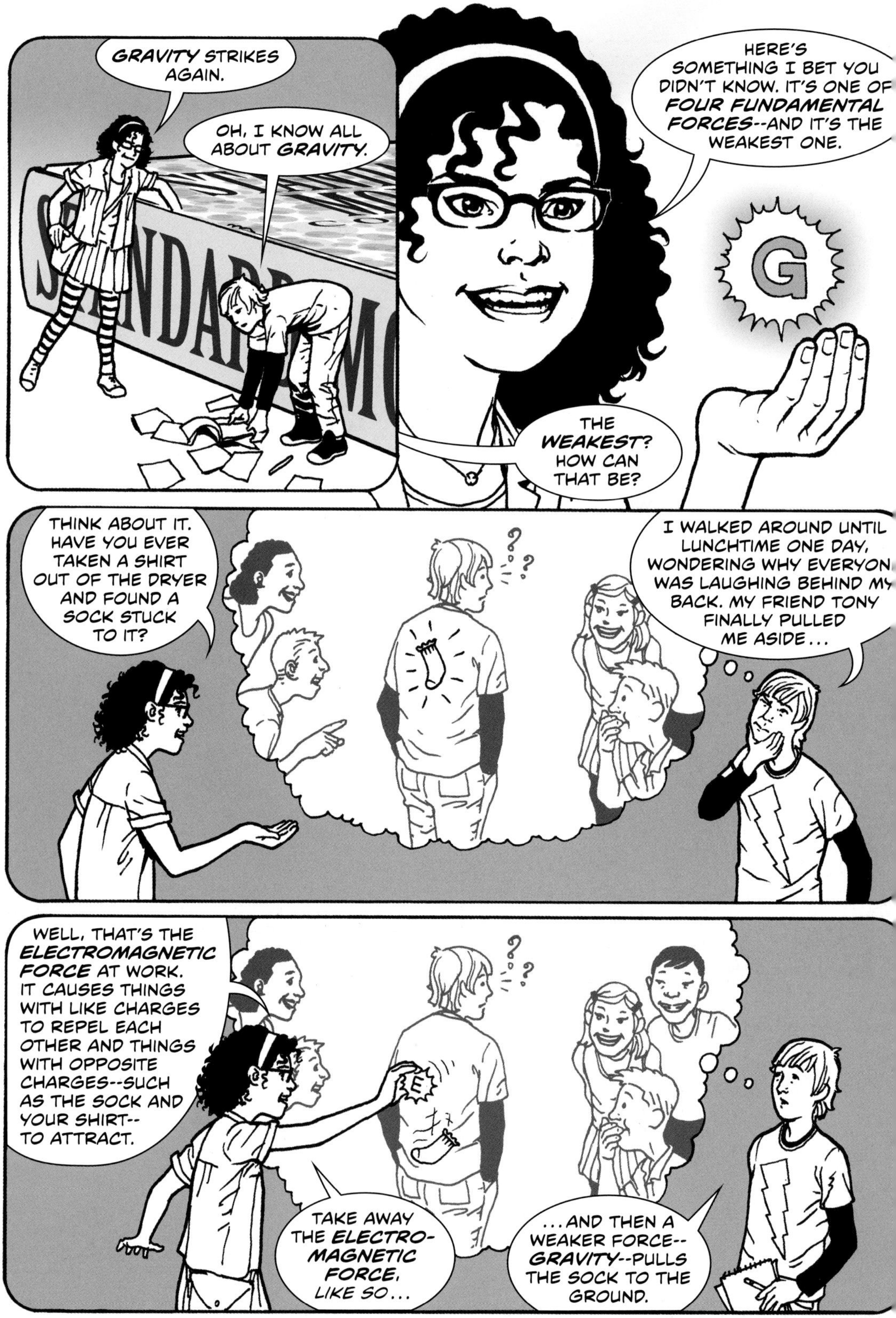
GRAVITY STRIKES AGAIN.
OH, I KNOW ALL ABOUT GRAVITY.
HERE'S SOMETHING I BET YOU DIDN'T KNOW. IT'S ONE OF FOUR FUNDAMENTAL FORCES--AND IT'S THE WEAKEST ONE.
G
THE WEAKEST? HOW CAN THAT BE?
THINK ABOUT IT. HAVE YOU EVER TAKEN A SHIRT OUT OF THE DRYER AND FOUND A SOCK STUCK TO IT?
I WALKED AROUND UNTIL LUNCHTIME ONE DAY, WONDERING WHY EVERYON WAS LAUGHING BEHIND MY BACK. MY FRIEND TONY FINALLY PULLED ME ASIDE...
WELL, THAT'S THE ELECTROMAGNETIC FORCE AT WORK. IT CAUSES THINGS WITH LIKE CHARGES TO REPEL EACH OTHER AND THINGS WITH OPPOSITE CHARGES--SUCH AS THE SOCK AND YOUR SHIRT--TO ATTRACT.
E
TAKE AWAY THE ELECTRO-MAGNETIC FORCE, LIKE SO...
...AND THEN A WEAKER FORCE--GRAVITY--PULLS THE SOCK TO THE GROUND.

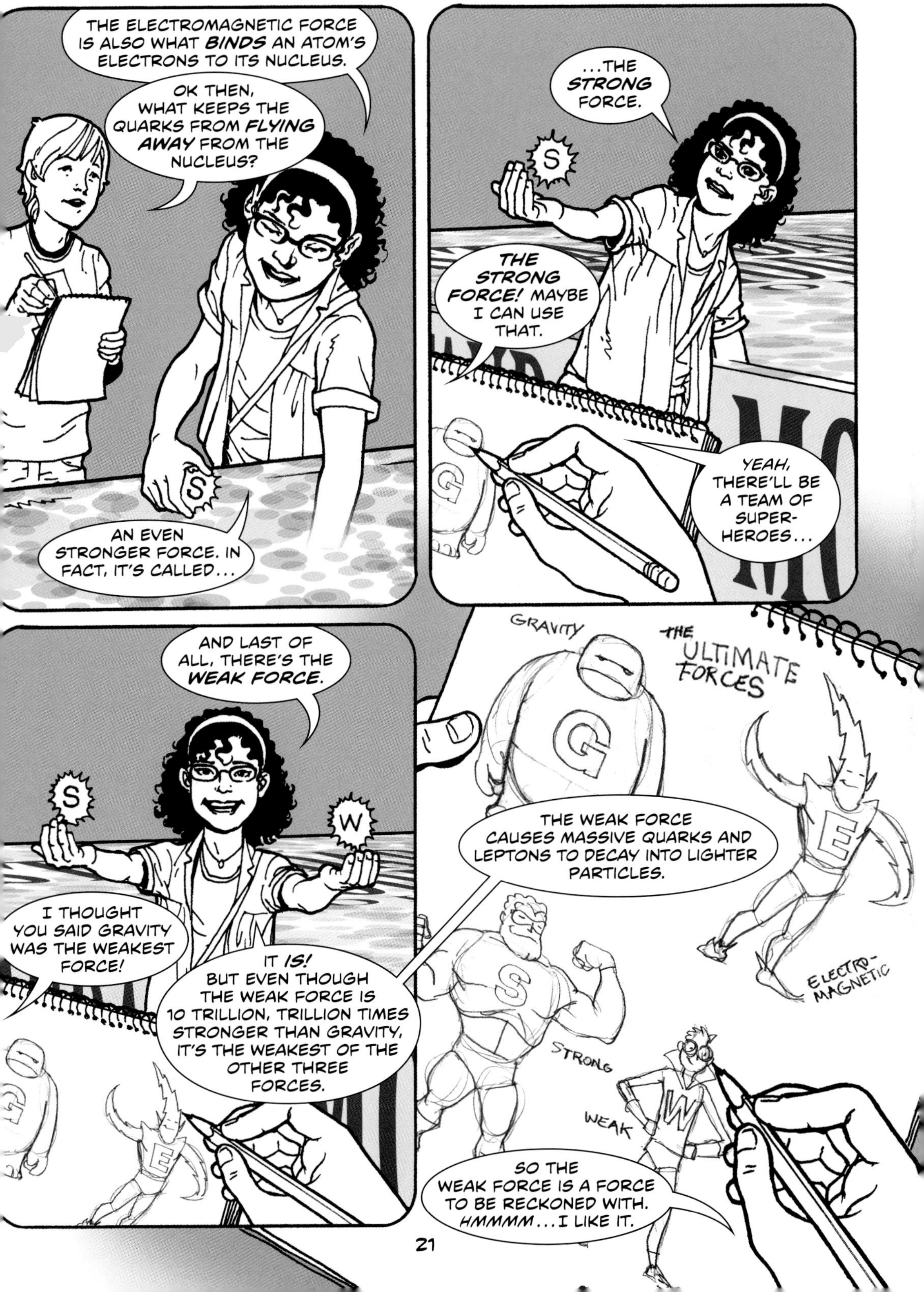
THE ELECTROMAGNETIC FORCE IS ALSO WHAT BINDS AN ATOM'S ELECTRONS TO ITS NUCLEUS.
OK THEN, WHAT KEEPS THE QUARKS FROM FLYING AWAY FROM THE NUCLEUS?
AN EVEN STRONGER FORCE. IN FACT, IT'S CALLED...
...THE STRONG FORCE.
THE STRONG FORCE! MAYBE I CAN USE THAT.
YEAH, THERE'LL BE A TEAM OF SUPER-HEROES...
AND LAST OF ALL, THERE'S THE WEAK FORCE.
I THOUGHT YOU SAID GRAVITY WAS THE WEAKEST FORCE!
IT IS! BUT EVEN THOUGH THE WEAK FORCE IS 10 TRILLION, TRILLION TIMES STRONGER THAN GRAVITY, IT'S THE WEAKEST OF THE OTHER THREE FORCES.
GRAVITY
THE ULTIMATE FORCES
THE WEAK FORCE CAUSES MASSIVE QUARKS AND LEPTONS TO DECAY INTO LIGHTER PARTICLES.
ELECTRO-MAGNETIC
STRONG
WEAK
SO THE WEAK FORCE IS A FORCE TO BE RECKONED WITH. HMMMM...I LIKE IT.

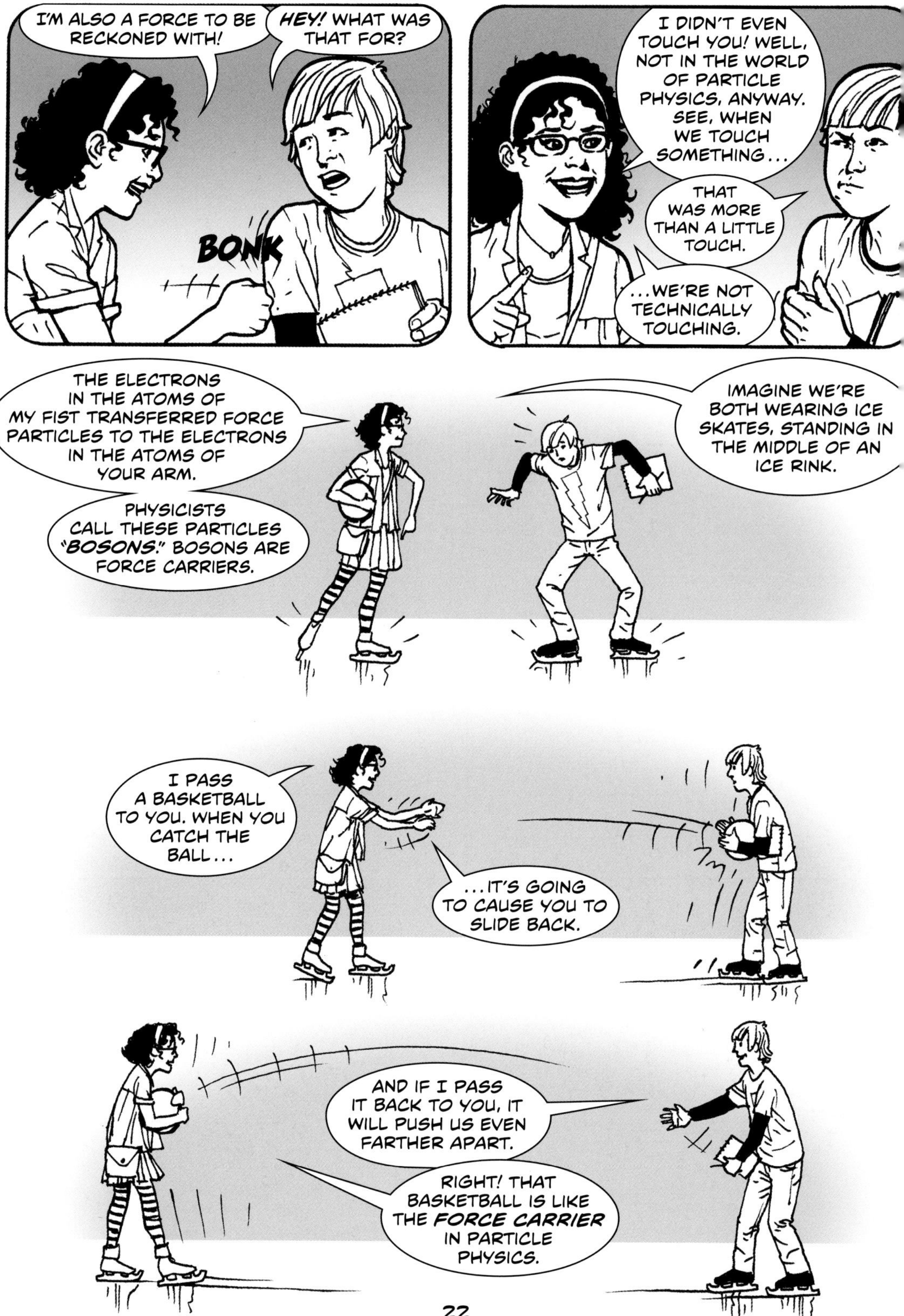
I'M ALSO A FORCE TO BE RECKONED WITH!
HEY! WHAT WAS THAT FOR?
BONK
I DIDN'T EVEN TOUCH YOU! WELL, NOT IN THE WORLD OF PARTICLE PHYSICS, ANYWAY. SEE, WHEN WE TOUCH SOMETHING...
THAT WAS MORE THAN A LITTLE TOUCH.
...WE'RE NOT TECHNICALLY TOUCHING.
THE ELECTRONS IN THE ATOMS OF MY FIST TRANSFERRED FORCE PARTICLES TO THE ELECTRONS IN THE ATOMS OF YOUR ARM.
PHYSICISTS CALL THESE PARTICLES "BOSONS." BOSONS ARE FORCE CARRIERS.
IMAGINE WE'RE BOTH WEARING ICE SKATES, STANDING IN THE MIDDLE OF AN ICE RINK.
I PASS A BASKETBALL TO YOU. WHEN YOU CATCH THE BALL...
...IT'S GOING TO CAUSE YOU TO SLIDE BACK.
AND IF I PASS IT BACK TO YOU, IT WILL PUSH US EVEN FARTHER APART.
RIGHT! THAT BASKETBALL IS LIKE THE FORCE CARRIER IN PARTICLE PHYSICS.

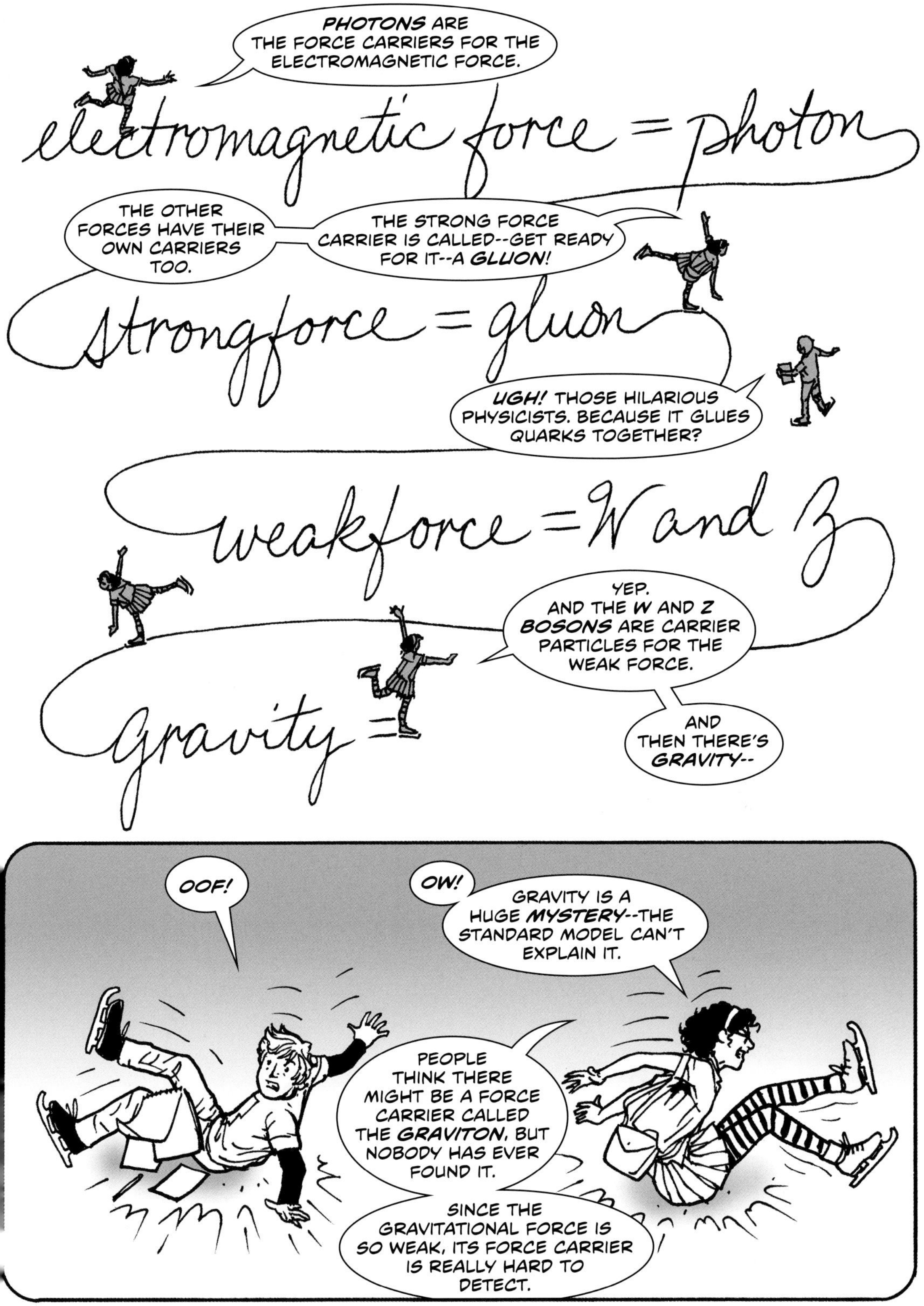
PHOTONS ARE THE FORCE CARRIERS FOR THE ELECTROMAGNETIC FORCE.
electromagnetic force = photon
THE OTHER FORCES HAVE THEIR OWN CARRIERS TOO.
THE STRONG FORCE CARRIER IS CALLED--GET READY FOR IT--A GLUON!
strongforce = gluon
UGH! THOSE HILARIOUS PHYSICISTS. BECAUSE IT GLUES QUARKS TOGETHER?
weakforce = W and Z
YEP. AND THE W AND Z BOSONS ARE CARRIER PARTICLES FOR THE WEAK FORCE.
AND THEN THERE'S GRAVITY--
gravity =
OOF!
OW!
GRAVITY IS A HUGE MYSTERY--THE STANDARD MODEL CAN'T EXPLAIN IT.
PEOPLE THINK THERE MIGHT BE A FORCE CARRIER CALLED THE GRAVITON, BUT NOBODY HAS EVER FOUND IT.
SINCE THE GRAVITATIONAL FORCE IS SO WEAK, ITS FORCE CARRIER IS REALLY HARD TO DETECT.

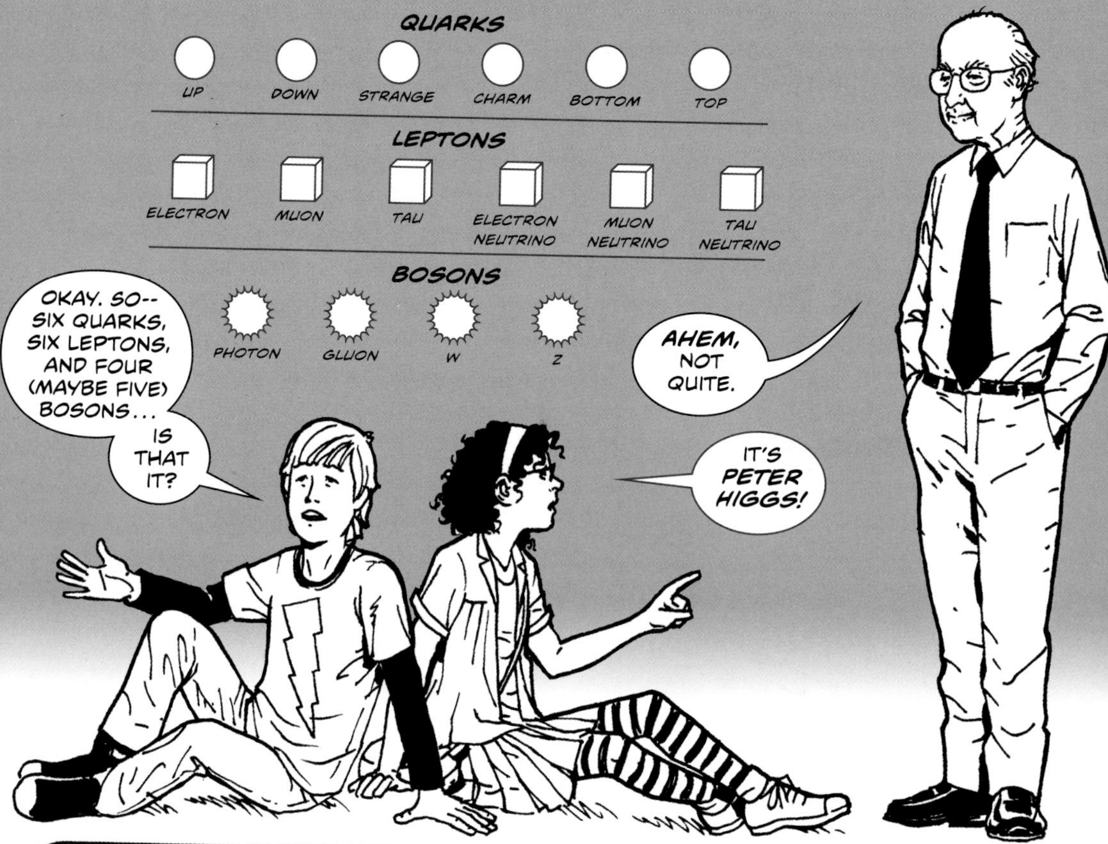
QUARKS
UP
DOWN
STRANGE
CHARM
BOTTOM
TOP
LEPTONS
ELECTRON
MUON
TAU
ELECTRON NEUTRINO
MUON NEUTRINO
TAU NEUTRINO
BOSONS
PHOTON
GLUON
W
Z
OKAY. SO-- SIX QUARKS, SIX LEPTONS, AND FOUR (MAYBE FIVE) BOSONS...
IS THAT IT?
AHEM, NOT QUITE.
IT'S PETER HIGGS!

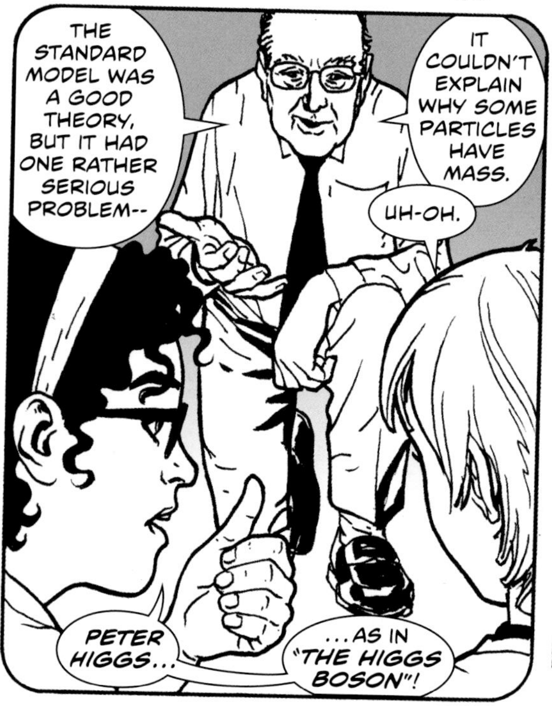
THE STANDARD MODEL WAS A GOOD THEORY, BUT IT HAD ONE RATHER SERIOUS PROBLEM--
IT COULDN'T EXPLAIN WHY SOME PARTICLES HAVE MASS.
UH-OH.
PETER HIGGS...
...AS IN "THE HIGGS BOSON"!

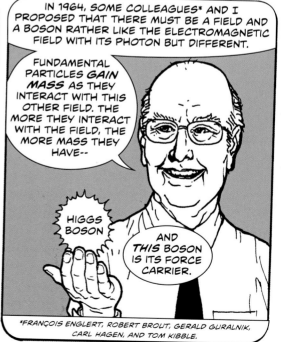

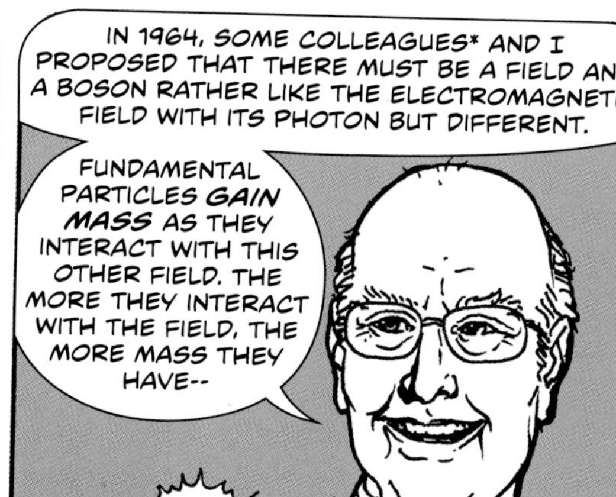
IN 1964, SOME COLLEAGUES* AND I PROPOSED THAT THERE MUST BE A FIELD AND A BOSON RATHER LIKE THE ELECTROMAGNETIC FIELD WITH ITS PHOTON BUT DIFFERENT.
FUNDAMENTAL PARTICLES GAIN MASS AS THEY INTERACT WITH THIS OTHER FIELD. THE MORE THEY INTERACT WITH THE FIELD, THE MORE MASS THEY HAVE--
HIGGS BOSON
AND THIS BOSON IS ITS FORCE CARRIER.

*FRANÇOIS ENGLERT, ROBERT BROUT, GERALD GURALNIK, CARL HAGEN, AND TOM KIBBLE.

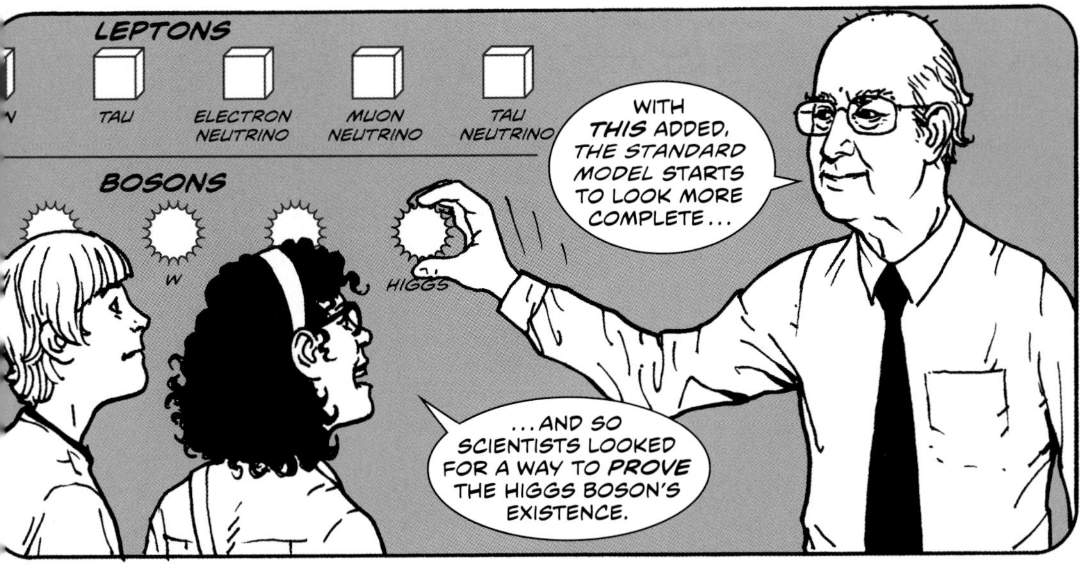
LEPTONS
TAU
ELECTRON NEUTRINO
MUON NEUTRINO
TAU NEUTRINO
BOSONS
W
HIGGS
WITH THIS ADDED, THE STANDARD MODEL STARTS TO LOOK MORE COMPLETE...
...AND SO SCIENTISTS LOOKED FOR A WAY TO PROVE THE HIGGS BOSON'S EXISTENCE.

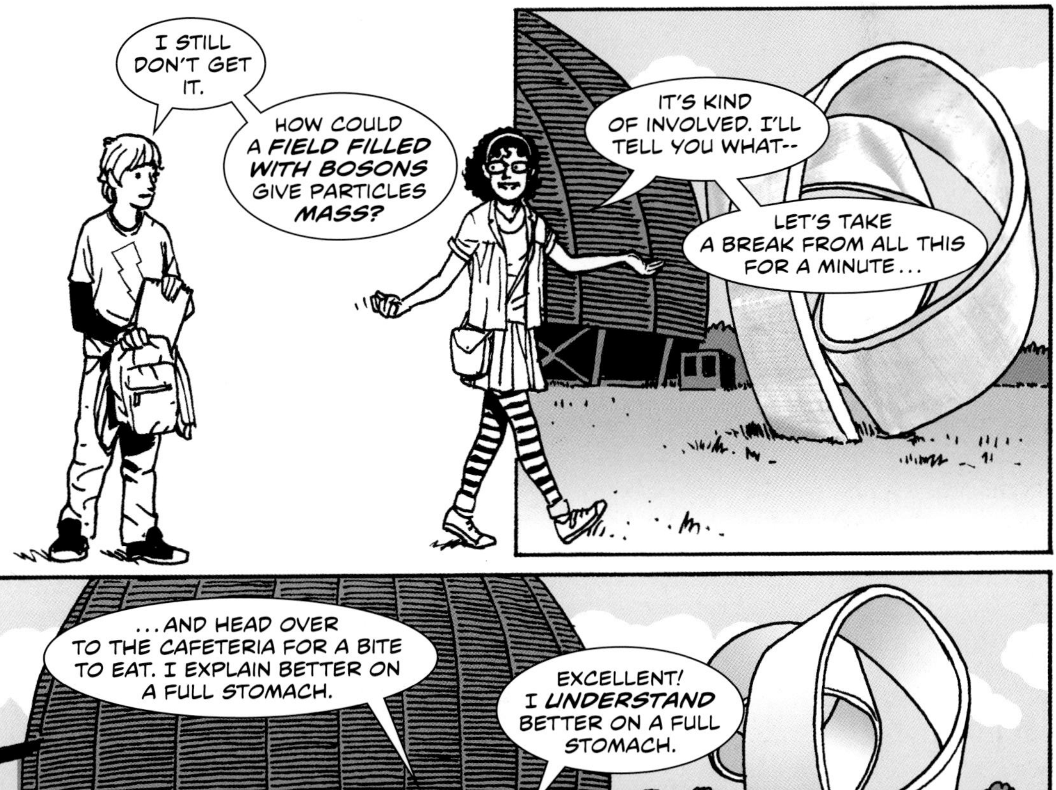
I STILL DON'T GET IT.
HOW COULD A FIELD FILLED WITH BOSONS GIVE PARTICLES MASS?
IT'S KIND OF INVOLVED. I'LL TELL YOU WHAT--
LET'S TAKE A BREAK FROM ALL THIS FOR A MINUTE...

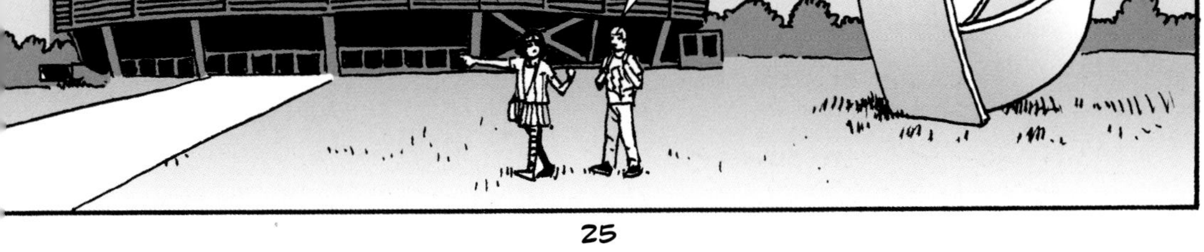
...AND HEAD OVER TO THE CAFETERIA FOR A BITE TO EAT. I EXPLAIN BETTER ON A FULL STOMACH.
EXCELLENT! I UNDERSTAND BETTER ON A FULL STOMACH.

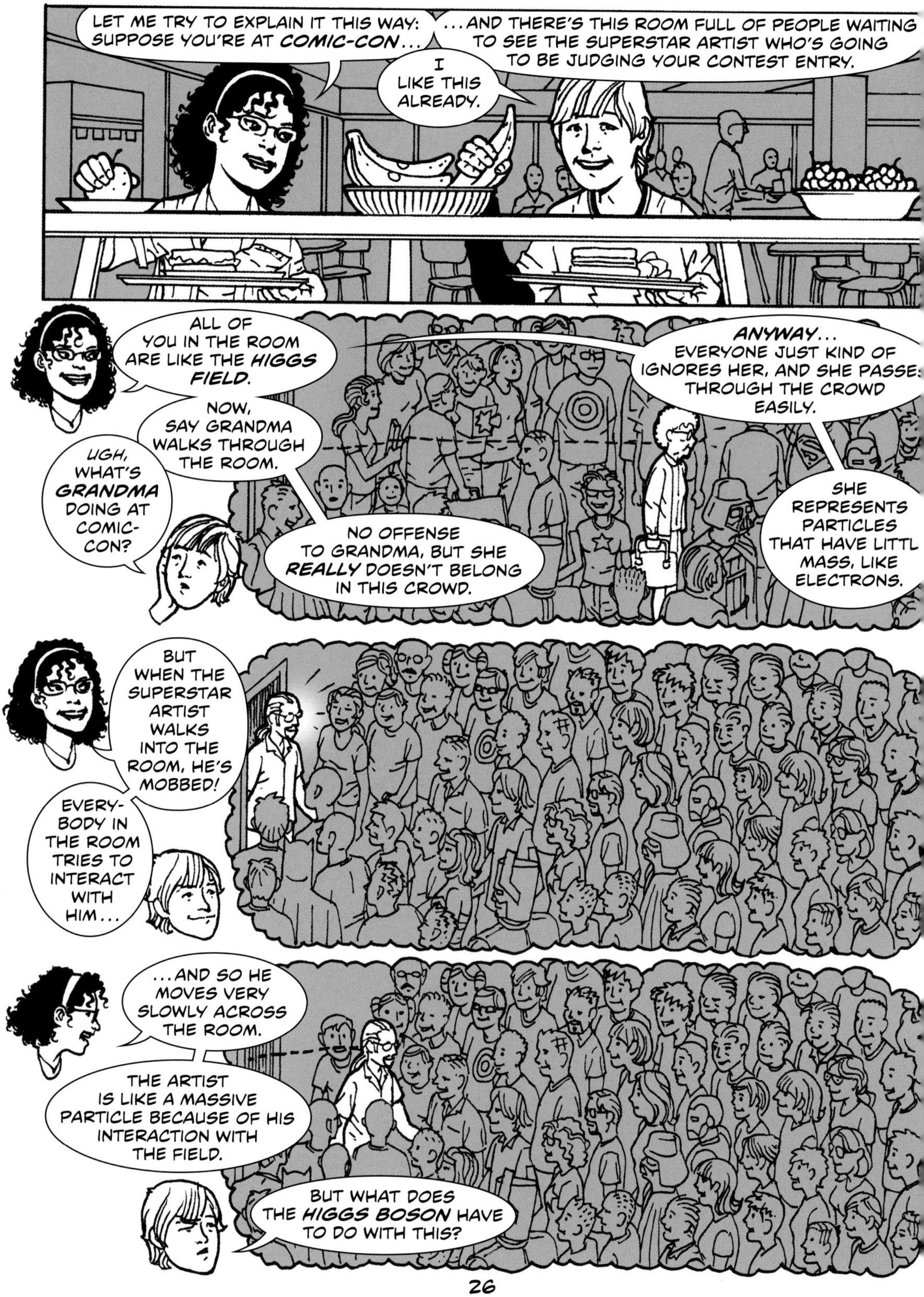
LET ME TRY TO EXPLAIN IT THIS WAY: SUPPOSE YOU'RE AT COMIC-CON...
I LIKE THIS ALREADY.
...AND THERE'S THIS ROOM FULL OF PEOPLE WAITING TO SEE THE SUPERSTAR ARTIST WHO'S GOING TO BE JUDGING YOUR CONTEST ENTRY.
ALL OF YOU IN THE ROOM ARE LIKE THE HIGGS FIELD.
NOW, SAY GRANDMA WALKS THROUGH THE ROOM.
UGH, WHAT'S GRANDMA DOING AT COMIC-CON?
NO OFFENSE TO GRANDMA, BUT SHE REALLY DOESN'T BELONG IN THIS CROWD.
ANYWAY... EVERYONE JUST KIND OF IGNORES HER, AND SHE PASSES THROUGH THE CROWD EASILY.
SHE REPRESENTS PARTICLES THAT HAVE LITTL MASS, LIKE ELECTRONS.
BUT WHEN THE SUPERSTAR ARTIST WALKS INTO THE ROOM, HE'S MOBBED!
EVERY-BODY IN THE ROOM TRIES TO INTERACT WITH HIM...
...AND SO HE MOVES VERY SLOWLY ACROSS THE ROOM.
THE ARTIST IS LIKE A MASSIVE PARTICLE BECAUSE OF HIS INTERACTION WITH THE FIELD.
BUT WHAT DOES THE HIGGS BOSON HAVE TO DO WITH THIS?

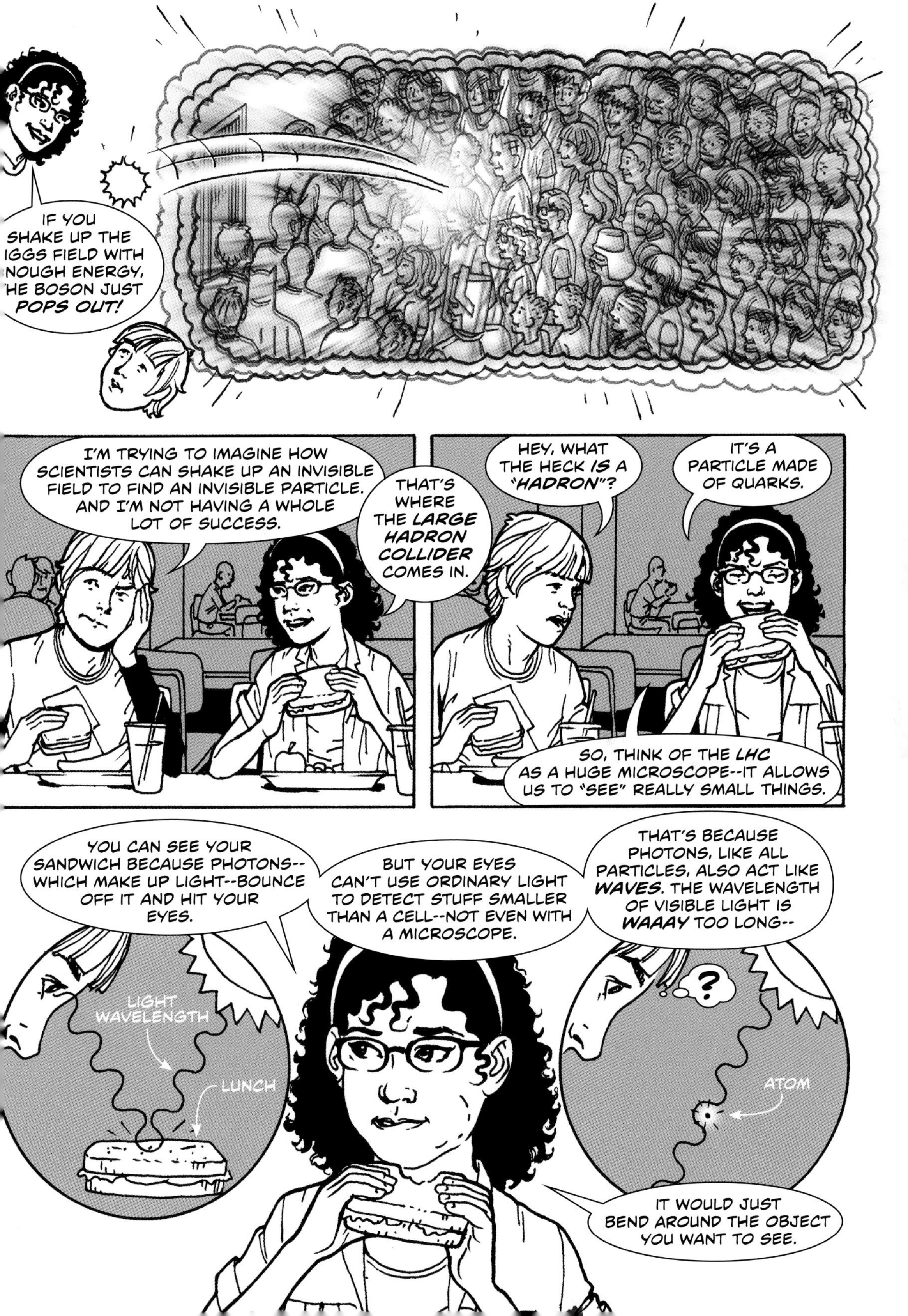
IF YOU SHAKE UP THE IGGS FIELD WITH NOUGH ENERGY, HE BOSON JUST *POPS OUT!*
I'M TRYING TO IMAGINE HOW SCIENTISTS CAN SHAKE UP AN INVISIBLE FIELD TO FIND AN INVISIBLE PARTICLE. AND I'M NOT HAVING A WHOLE LOT OF SUCCESS.
THAT'S WHERE THE *LARGE HADRON COLLIDER* COMES IN.
HEY, WHAT THE HECK *IS* A "*HADRON*"?
IT'S A PARTICLE MADE OF QUARKS.
SO, THINK OF THE *LHC* AS A HUGE MICROSCOPE--IT ALLOWS US TO "SEE" REALLY SMALL THINGS.
YOU CAN SEE YOUR SANDWICH BECAUSE PHOTONS--WHICH MAKE UP LIGHT--BOUNCE OFF IT AND HIT YOUR EYES.
LIGHT WAVELENGTH
LUNCH
BUT YOUR EYES CAN'T USE ORDINARY LIGHT TO DETECT STUFF SMALLER THAN A CELL--NOT EVEN WITH A MICROSCOPE.
THAT'S BECAUSE PHOTONS, LIKE ALL PARTICLES, ALSO ACT LIKE *WAVES*. THE WAVELENGTH OF VISIBLE LIGHT IS *WAAAY* TOO LONG--
?
ATOM
IT WOULD JUST BEND AROUND THE OBJECT YOU WANT TO SEE.

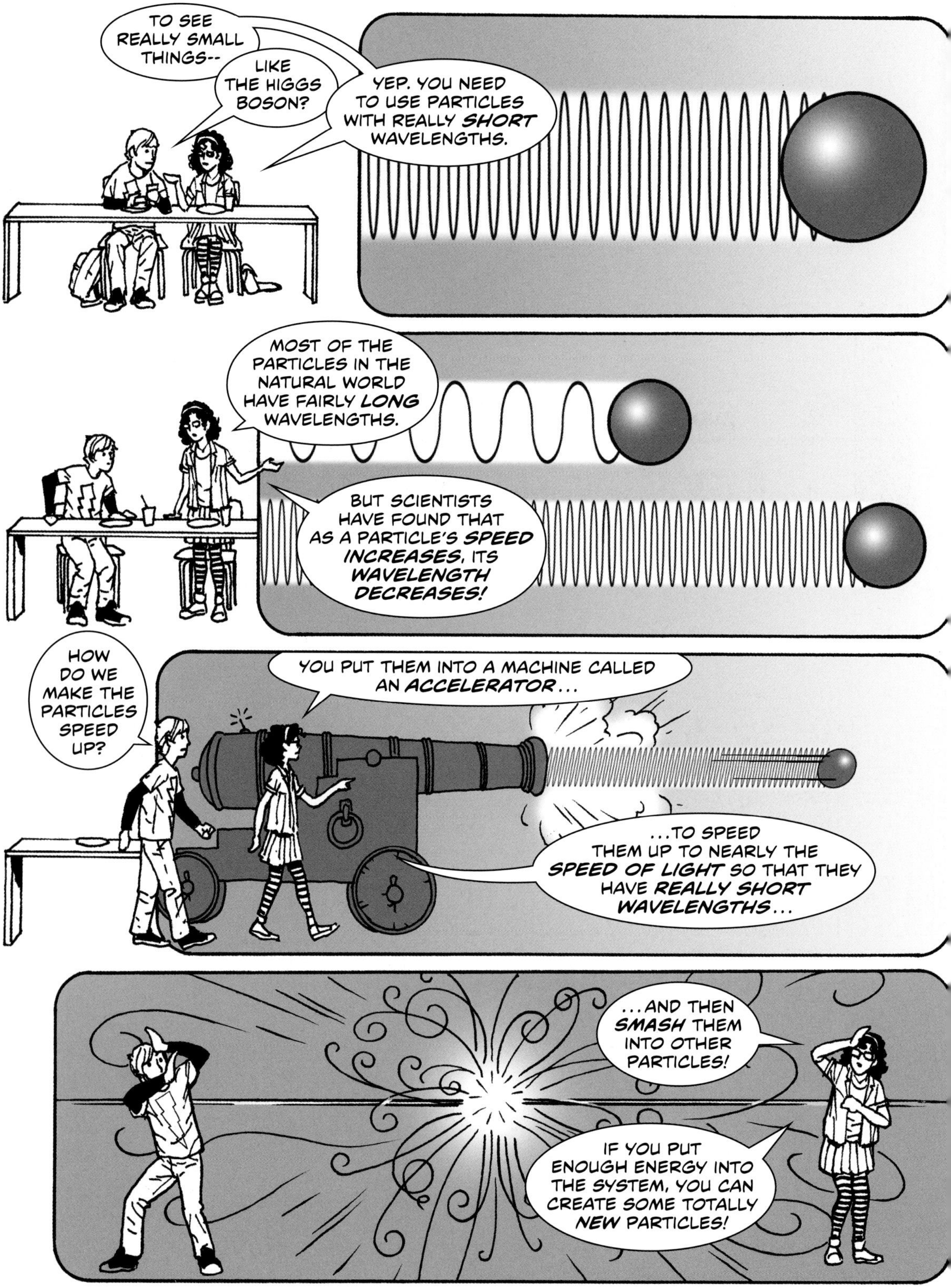
TO SEE REALLY SMALL THINGS--
LIKE THE HIGGS BOSON?
YEP. YOU NEED TO USE PARTICLES WITH REALLY SHORT WAVELENGTHS.
MOST OF THE PARTICLES IN THE NATURAL WORLD HAVE FAIRLY LONG WAVELENGTHS.
BUT SCIENTISTS HAVE FOUND THAT AS A PARTICLE'S SPEED INCREASES, ITS WAVELENGTH DECREASES!
HOW DO WE MAKE THE PARTICLES SPEED UP?
YOU PUT THEM INTO A MACHINE CALLED AN ACCELERATOR...
...TO SPEED THEM UP TO NEARLY THE SPEED OF LIGHT SO THAT THEY HAVE REALLY SHORT WAVELENGTHS...
...AND THEN SMASH THEM INTO OTHER PARTICLES!
IF YOU PUT ENOUGH ENERGY INTO THE SYSTEM, YOU CAN CREATE SOME TOTALLY NEW PARTICLES!

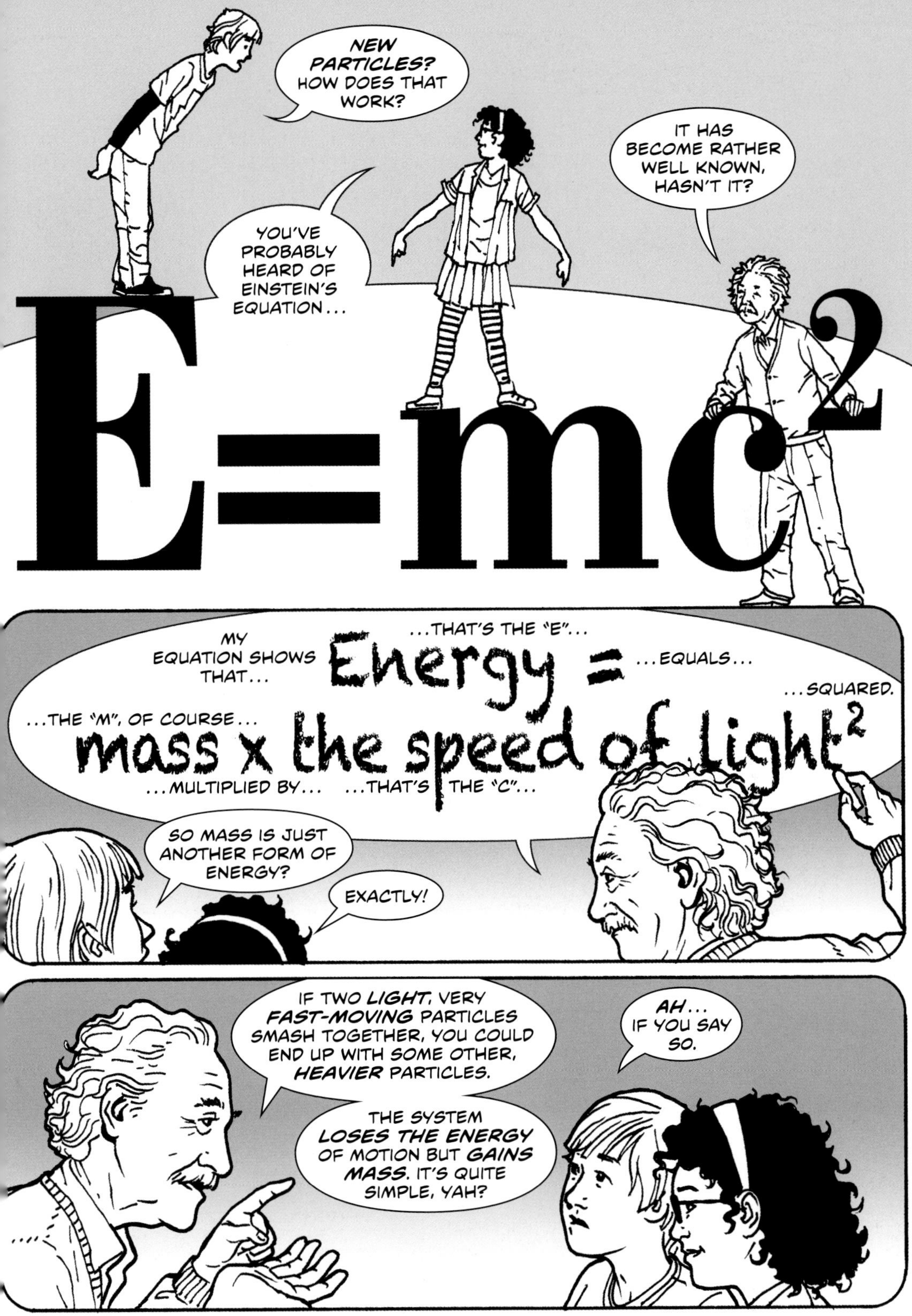
NEW PARTICLES? HOW DOES THAT WORK?
YOU'VE PROBABLY HEARD OF EINSTEIN'S EQUATION...
IT HAS BECOME RATHER WELL KNOWN, HASN'T IT?
E=mc²
MY EQUATION SHOWS THAT...
...THAT'S THE "E"...
Energy =
...EQUALS...
...THE "M", OF COURSE...
mass x the speed of light²
...SQUARED.
...MULTIPLIED BY...
...THAT'S THE "C"...
SO MASS IS JUST ANOTHER FORM OF ENERGY?
EXACTLY!
IF TWO LIGHT, VERY FAST-MOVING PARTICLES SMASH TOGETHER, YOU COULD END UP WITH SOME OTHER, HEAVIER PARTICLES.
THE SYSTEM LOSES THE ENERGY OF MOTION BUT GAINS MASS. IT'S QUITE SIMPLE, YAH?
AH... IF YOU SAY SO.

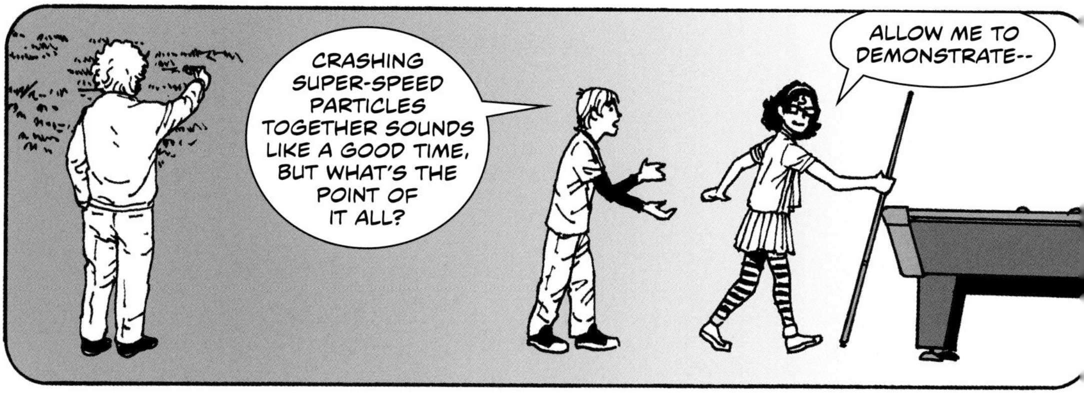
CRASHING SUPER-SPEED PARTICLES TOGETHER SOUNDS LIKE A GOOD TIME, BUT WHAT'S THE POINT OF IT ALL?
ALLOW ME TO DEMONSTRATE--

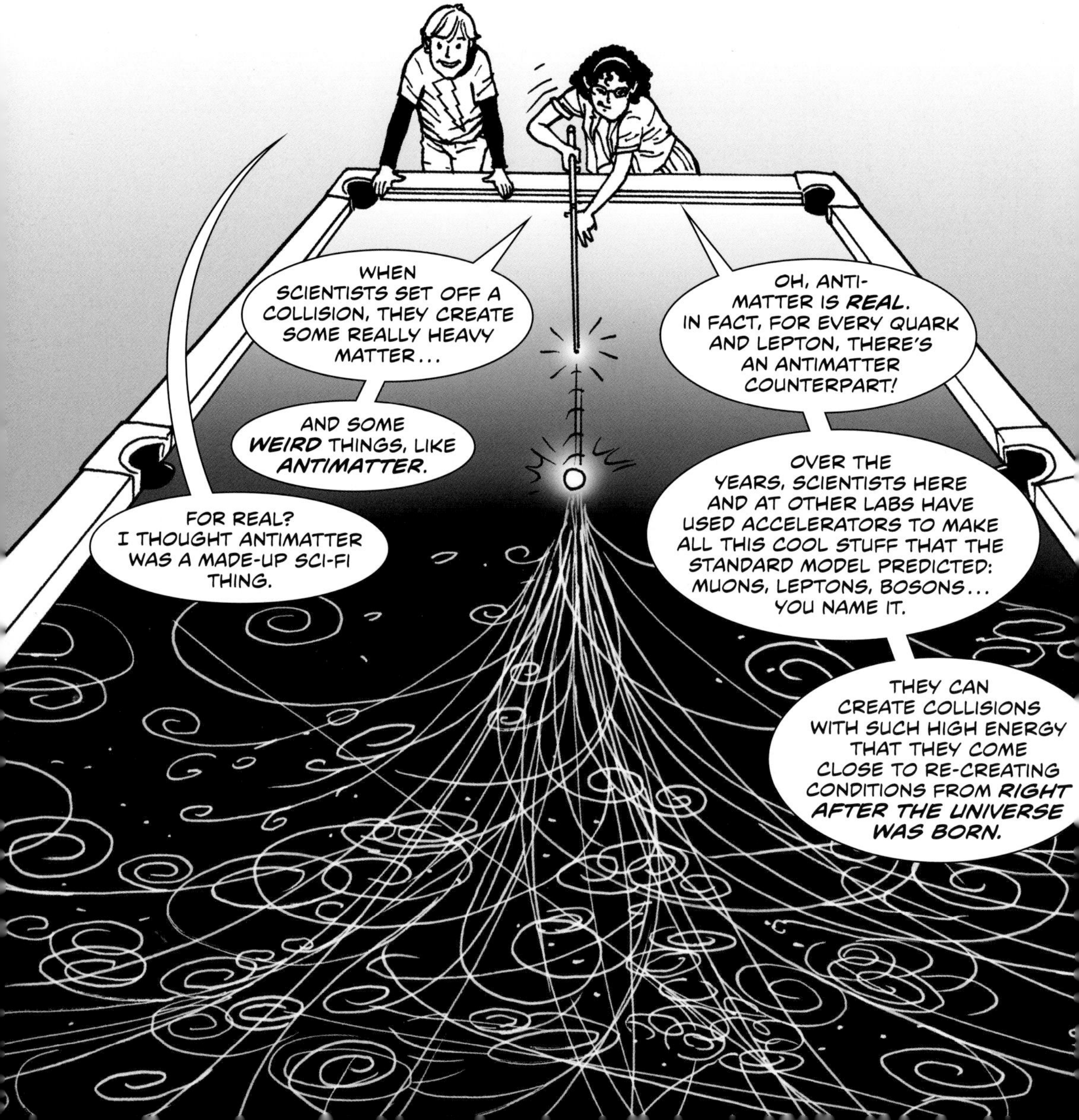
WHEN SCIENTISTS SET OFF A COLLISION, THEY CREATE SOME REALLY HEAVY MATTER...
AND SOME ***WEIRD*** THINGS, LIKE ***ANTIMATTER***.
FOR REAL? I THOUGHT ANTIMATTER WAS A MADE-UP SCI-FI THING.
OH, ANTI-MATTER IS ***REAL***. IN FACT, FOR EVERY QUARK AND LEPTON, THERE'S AN ANTIMATTER COUNTERPART!
OVER THE YEARS, SCIENTISTS HERE AND AT OTHER LABS HAVE USED ACCELERATORS TO MAKE ALL THIS COOL STUFF THAT THE STANDARD MODEL PREDICTED: MUONS, LEPTONS, BOSONS... YOU NAME IT.
THEY CAN CREATE COLLISIONS WITH SUCH HIGH ENERGY THAT THEY COME CLOSE TO RE-CREATING CONDITIONS FROM ***RIGHT AFTER THE UNIVERSE WAS BORN.***

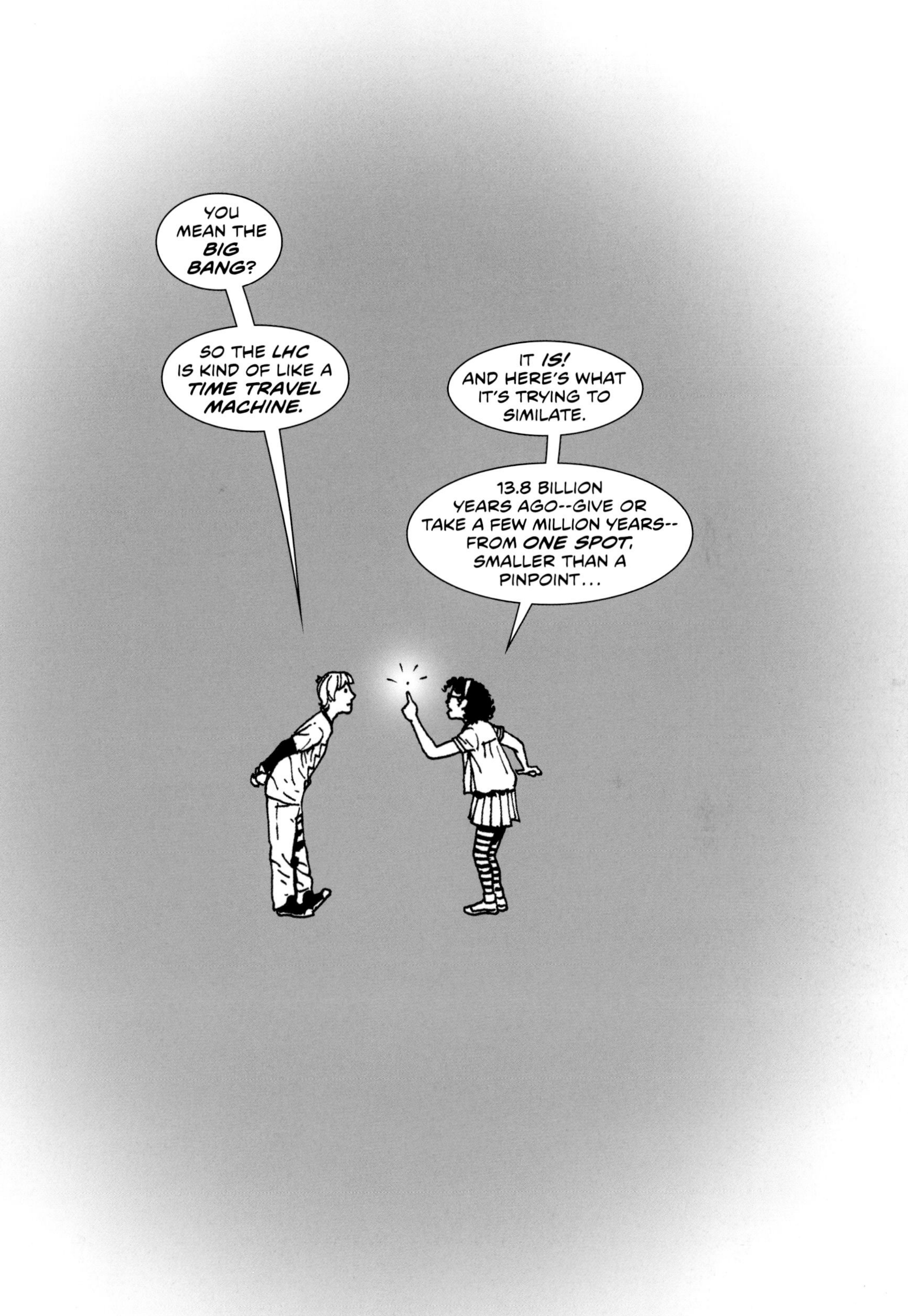
YOU MEAN THE BIG BANG?
SO THE LHC IS KIND OF LIKE A TIME TRAVEL MACHINE.
IT IS! AND HERE'S WHAT IT'S TRYING TO SIMILATE.
13.8 BILLION YEARS AGO--GIVE OR TAKE A FEW MILLION YEARS--FROM ONE SPOT, SMALLER THAN A PINPOINT...

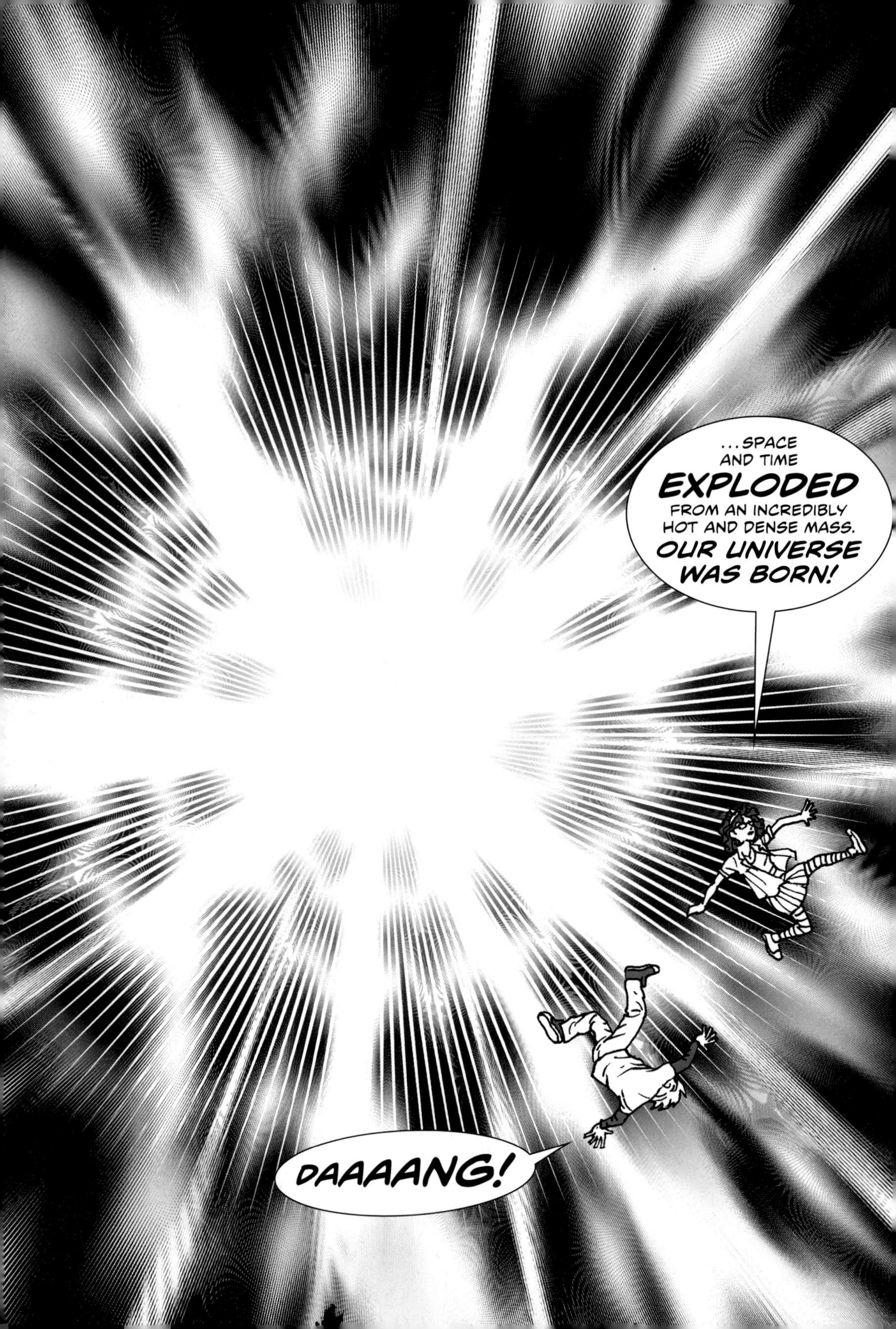
...SPACE AND TIME EXPLODED FROM AN INCREDIBLY HOT AND DENSE MASS. OUR UNIVERSE WAS BORN!
DAAAANG!

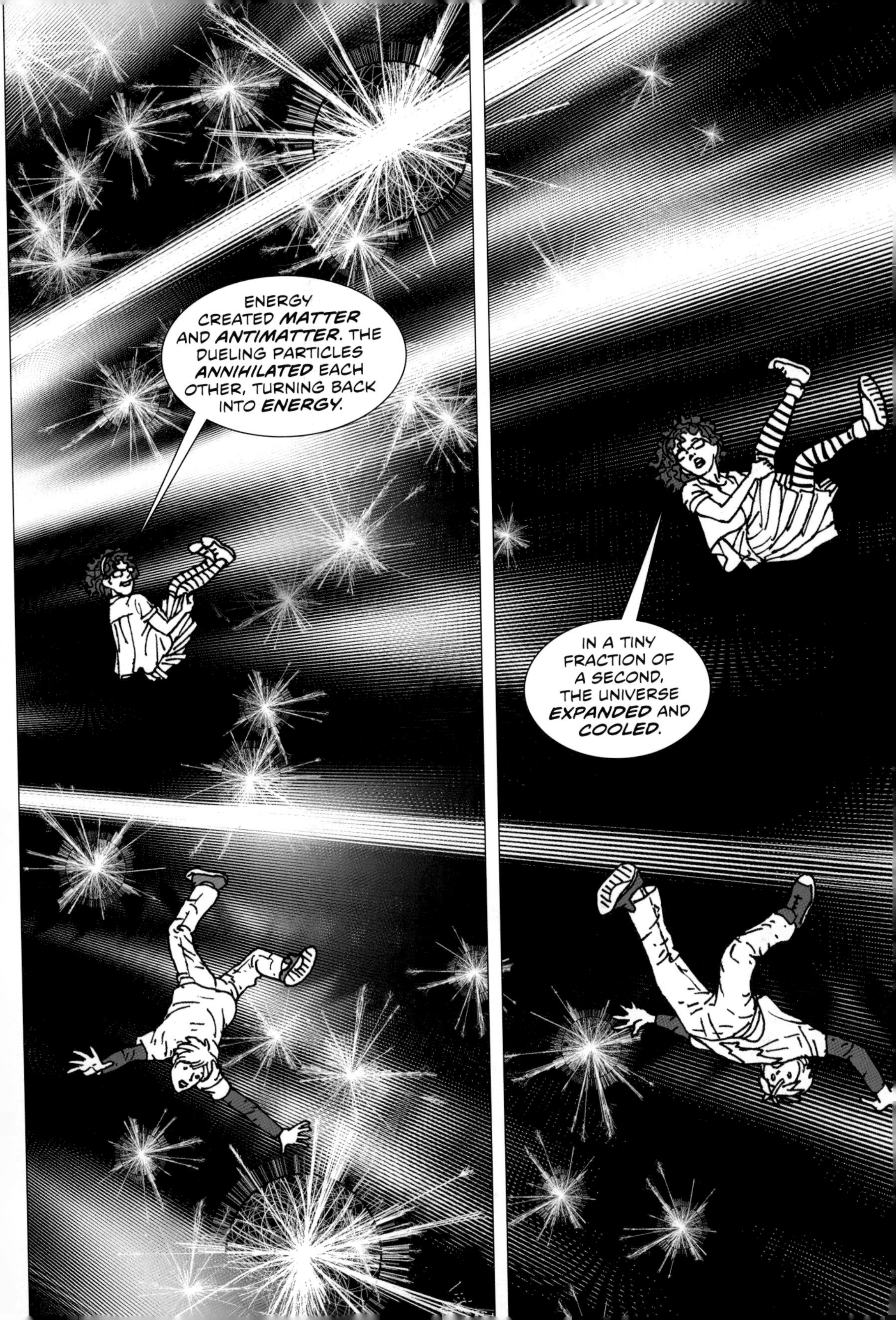
ENERGY CREATED MATTER AND ANTIMATTER. THE DUELING PARTICLES ANNIHILATED EACH OTHER, TURNING BACK INTO ENERGY.
IN A TINY FRACTION OF A SECOND, THE UNIVERSE EXPANDED AND COOLED.

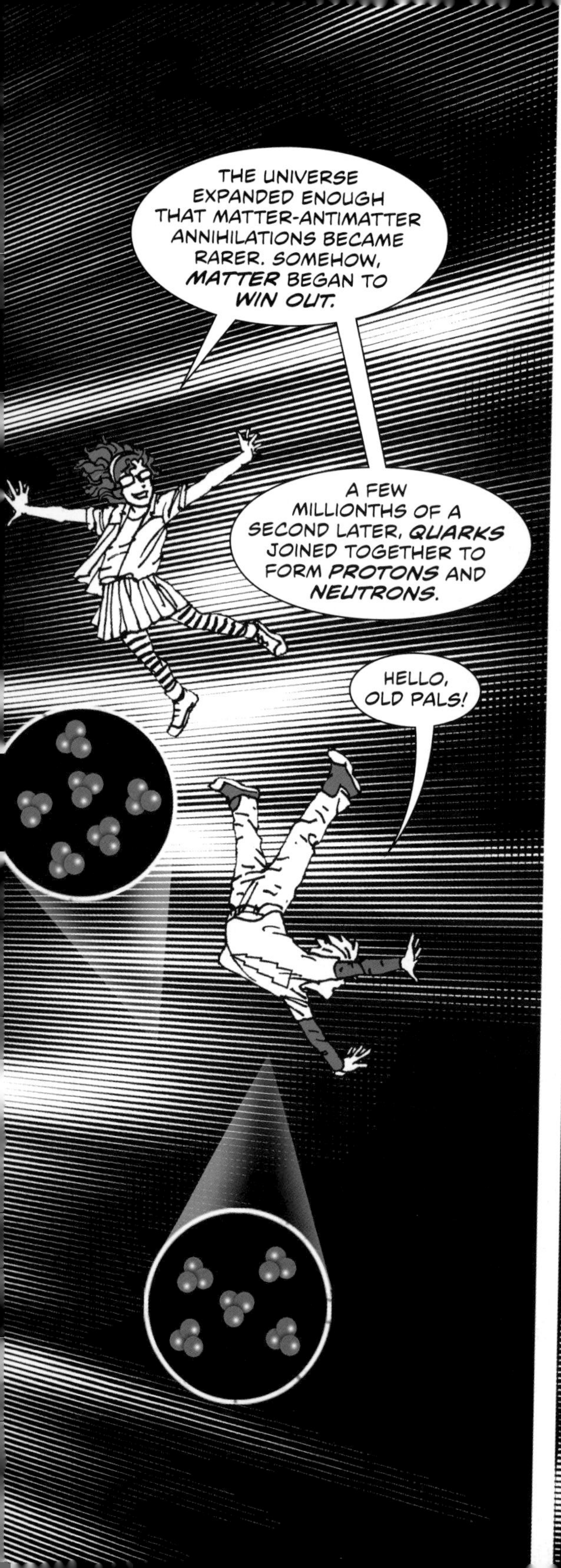
THE UNIVERSE EXPANDED ENOUGH THAT MATTER-ANTIMATTER ANNIHILATIONS BECAME RARER. SOMEHOW, **MATTER** BEGAN TO **WIN OUT.**
A FEW MILLIONTHS OF A SECOND LATER, **QUARKS** JOINED TOGETHER TO FORM **PROTONS** AND **NEUTRONS**.
HELLO, OLD PALS!

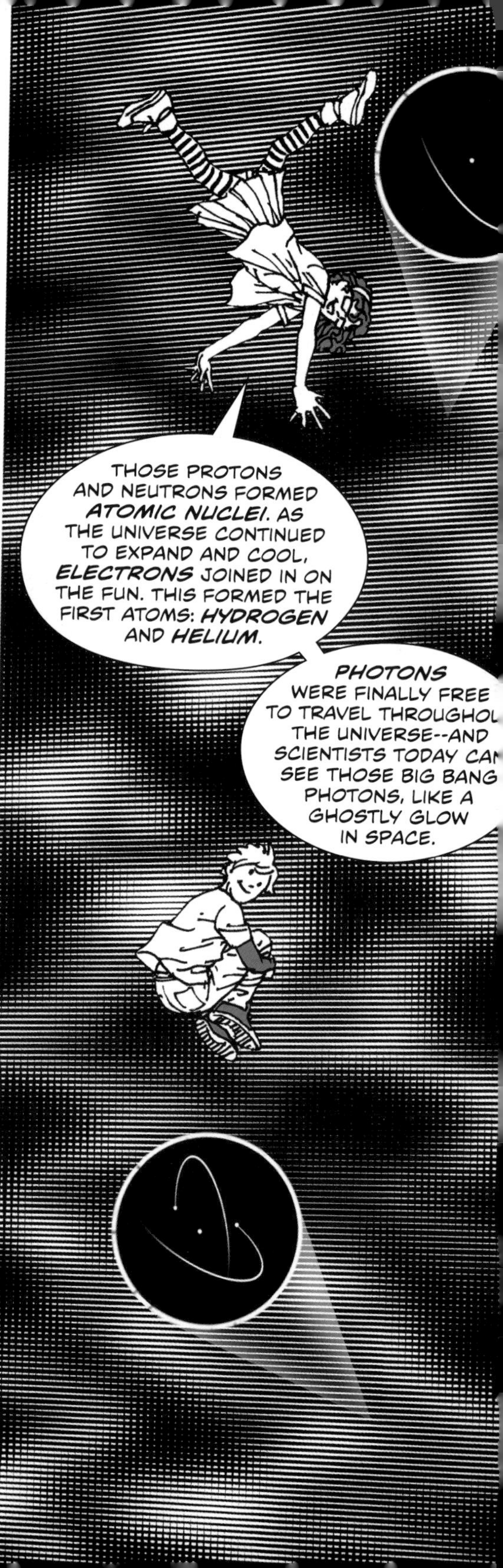
THOSE PROTONS AND NEUTRONS FORMED **ATOMIC NUCLEI**. AS THE UNIVERSE CONTINUED TO EXPAND AND COOL, **ELECTRONS** JOINED IN ON THE FUN. THIS FORMED THE FIRST ATOMS: **HYDROGEN** AND **HELIUM**.
PHOTONS WERE FINALLY FREE TO TRAVEL THROUGHOU THE UNIVERSE--AND SCIENTISTS TODAY CAN SEE THOSE BIG BANG PHOTONS, LIKE A GHOSTLY GLOW IN SPACE.

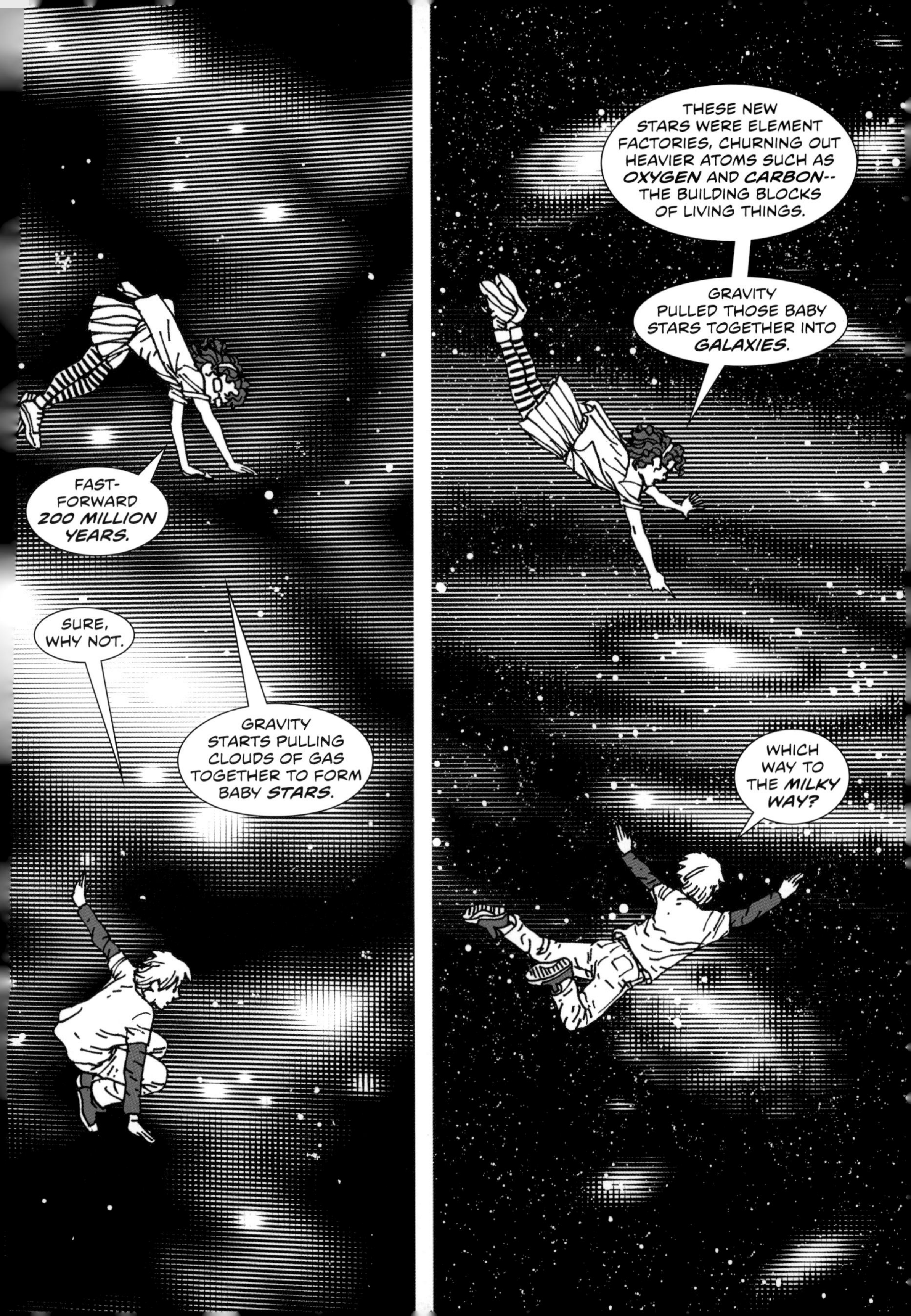
FAST-FORWARD 200 MILLION YEARS.
SURE, WHY NOT.
GRAVITY STARTS PULLING CLOUDS OF GAS TOGETHER TO FORM BABY STARS.
THESE NEW STARS WERE ELEMENT FACTORIES, CHURNING OUT HEAVIER ATOMS SUCH AS OXYGEN AND CARBON--THE BUILDING BLOCKS OF LIVING THINGS.
GRAVITY PULLED THOSE BABY STARS TOGETHER INTO GALAXIES.
WHICH WAY TO THE MILKY WAY?

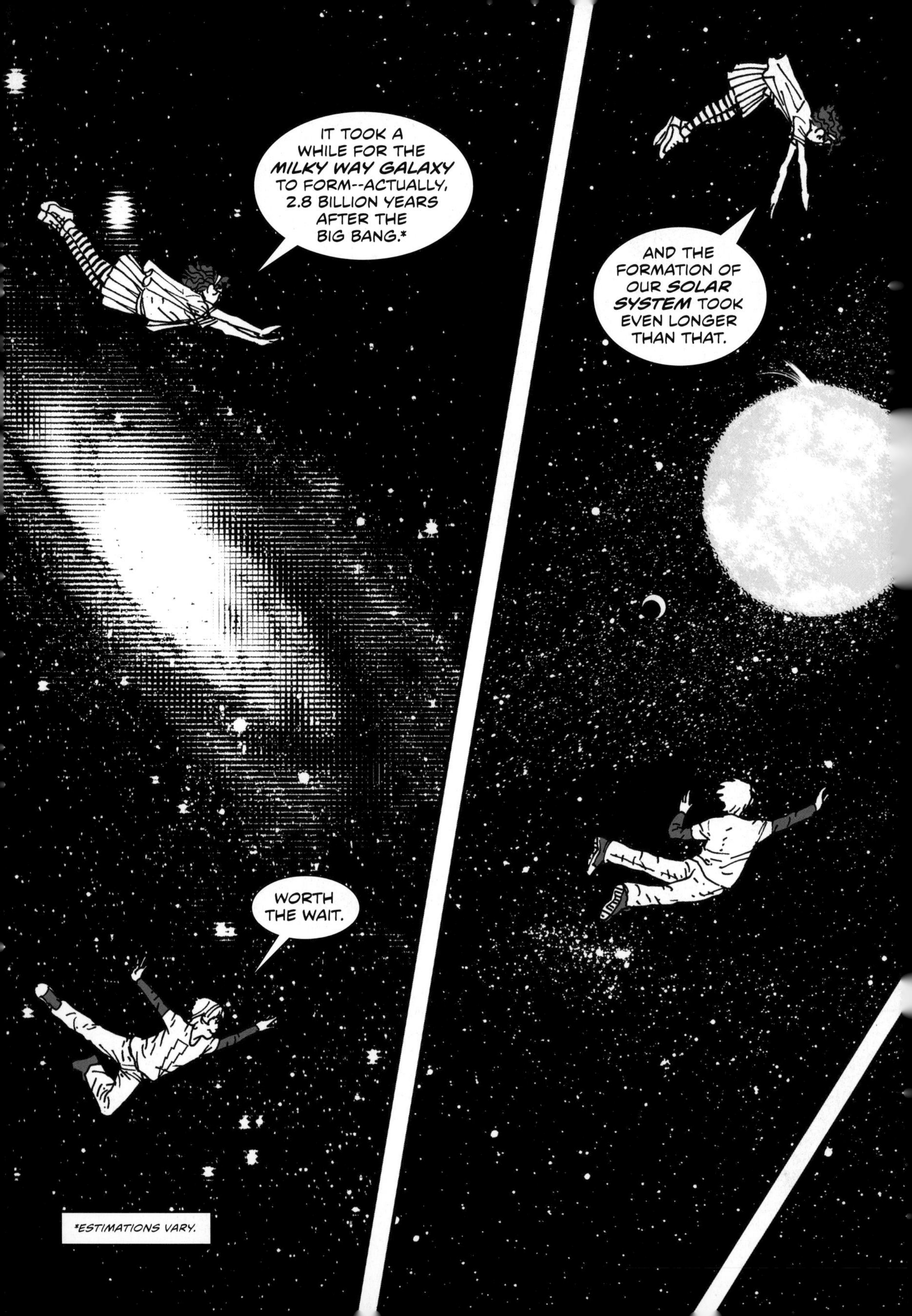

IT TOOK A WHILE FOR THE MILKY WAY GALAXY TO FORM--ACTUALLY, 2.8 BILLION YEARS AFTER THE BIG BANG.*
WORTH THE WAIT.
AND THE FORMATION OF OUR SOLAR SYSTEM TOOK EVEN LONGER THAN THAT.
*ESTIMATIONS VARY.

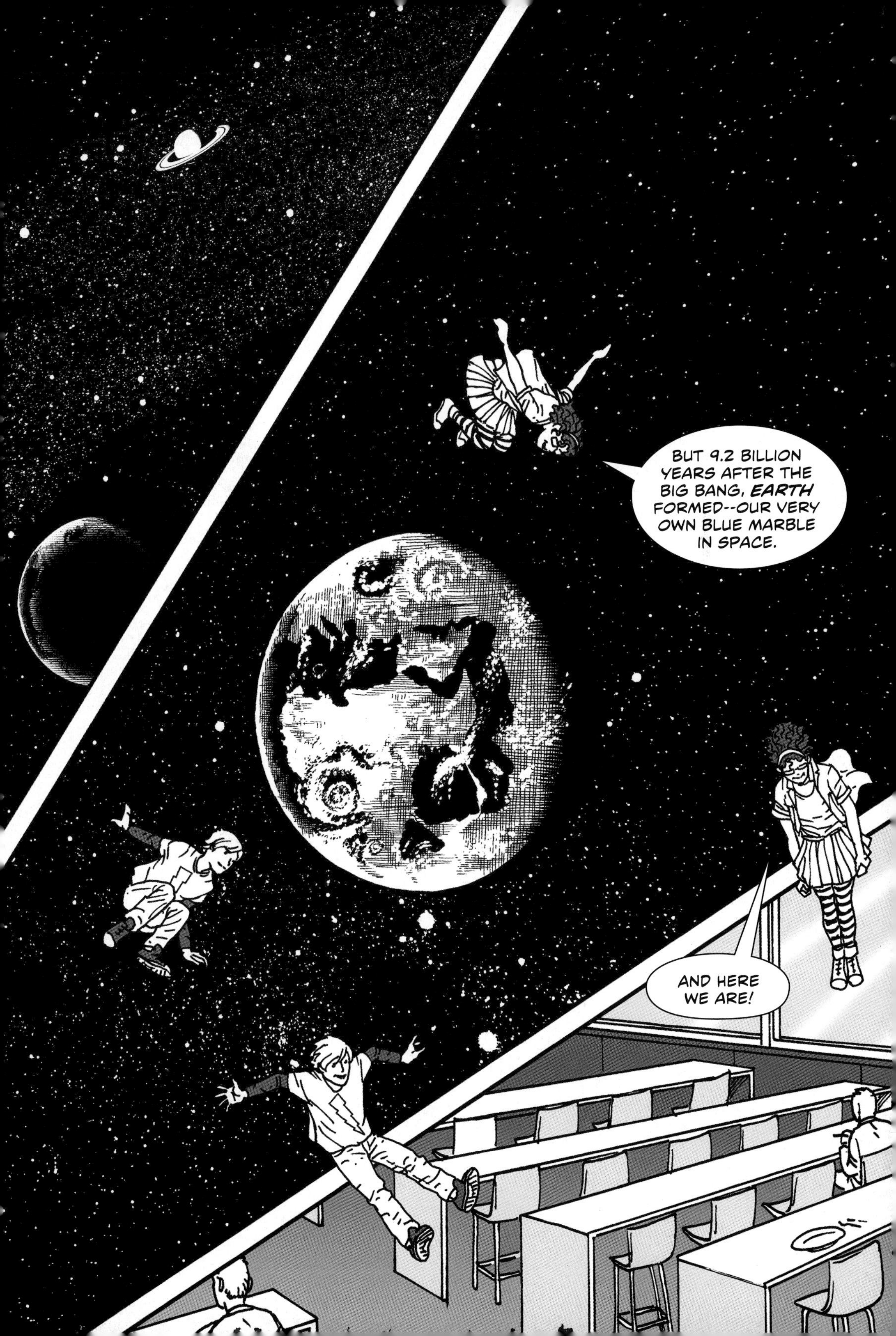
BUT 9.2 BILLION YEARS AFTER THE BIG BANG, *EARTH* FORMED--OUR VERY OWN BLUE MARBLE IN SPACE.
AND HERE WE ARE!

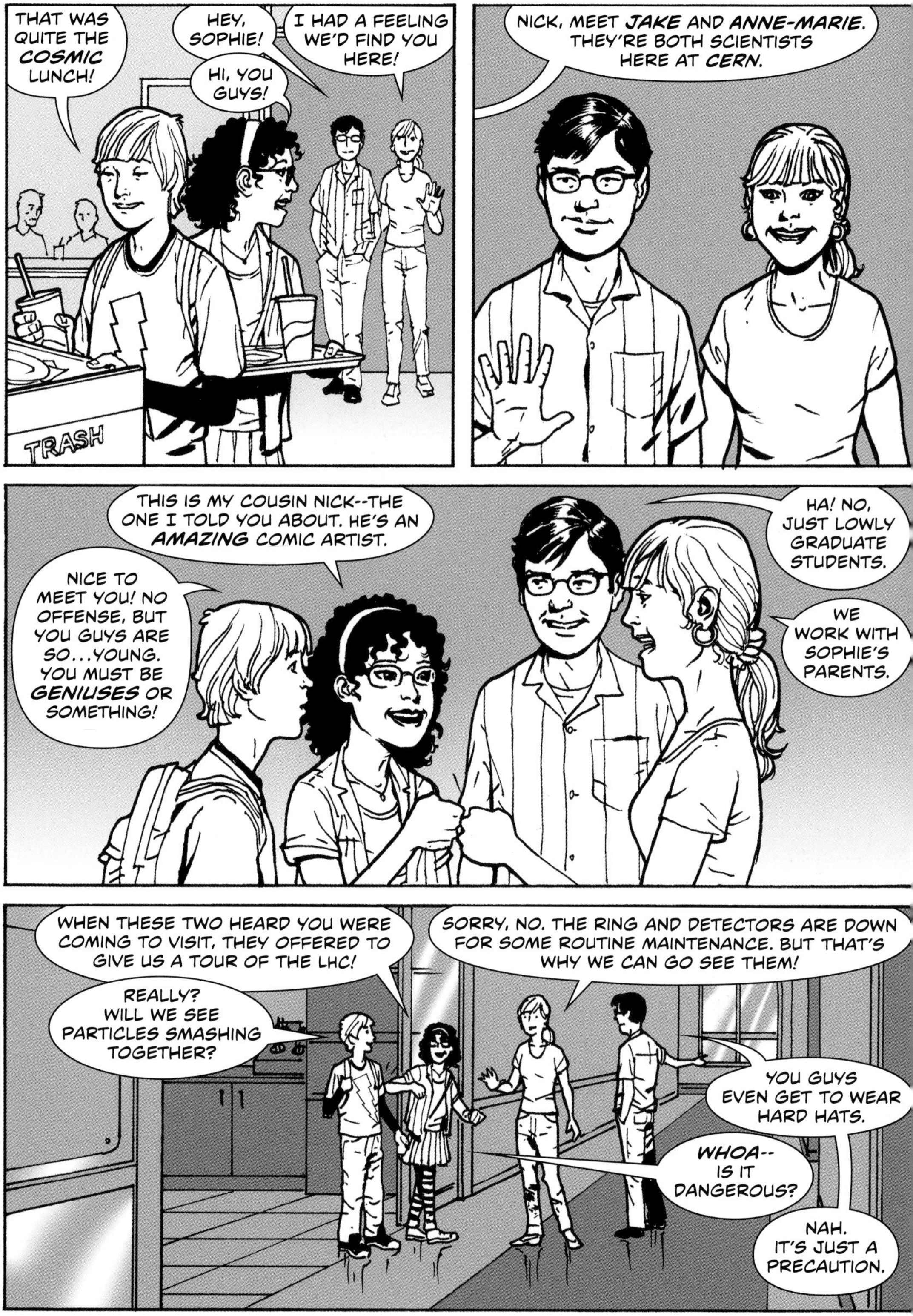
THAT WAS QUITE THE COSMIC LUNCH!
HEY, SOPHIE!
HI, YOU GUYS!
I HAD A FEELING WE'D FIND YOU HERE!
TRASH
NICK, MEET JAKE AND ANNE-MARIE. THEY'RE BOTH SCIENTISTS HERE AT CERN.
THIS IS MY COUSIN NICK--THE ONE I TOLD YOU ABOUT. HE'S AN AMAZING COMIC ARTIST.
NICE TO MEET YOU! NO OFFENSE, BUT YOU GUYS ARE SO...YOUNG. YOU MUST BE GENIUSES OR SOMETHING!
HA! NO, JUST LOWLY GRADUATE STUDENTS.
WE WORK WITH SOPHIE'S PARENTS.
WHEN THESE TWO HEARD YOU WERE COMING TO VISIT, THEY OFFERED TO GIVE US A TOUR OF THE LHC!
REALLY? WILL WE SEE PARTICLES SMASHING TOGETHER?
SORRY, NO. THE RING AND DETECTORS ARE DOWN FOR SOME ROUTINE MAINTENANCE. BUT THAT'S WHY WE CAN GO SEE THEM!
YOU GUYS EVEN GET TO WEAR HARD HATS.
WHOA-- IS IT DANGEROUS?
NAH. IT'S JUST A PRECAUTION.

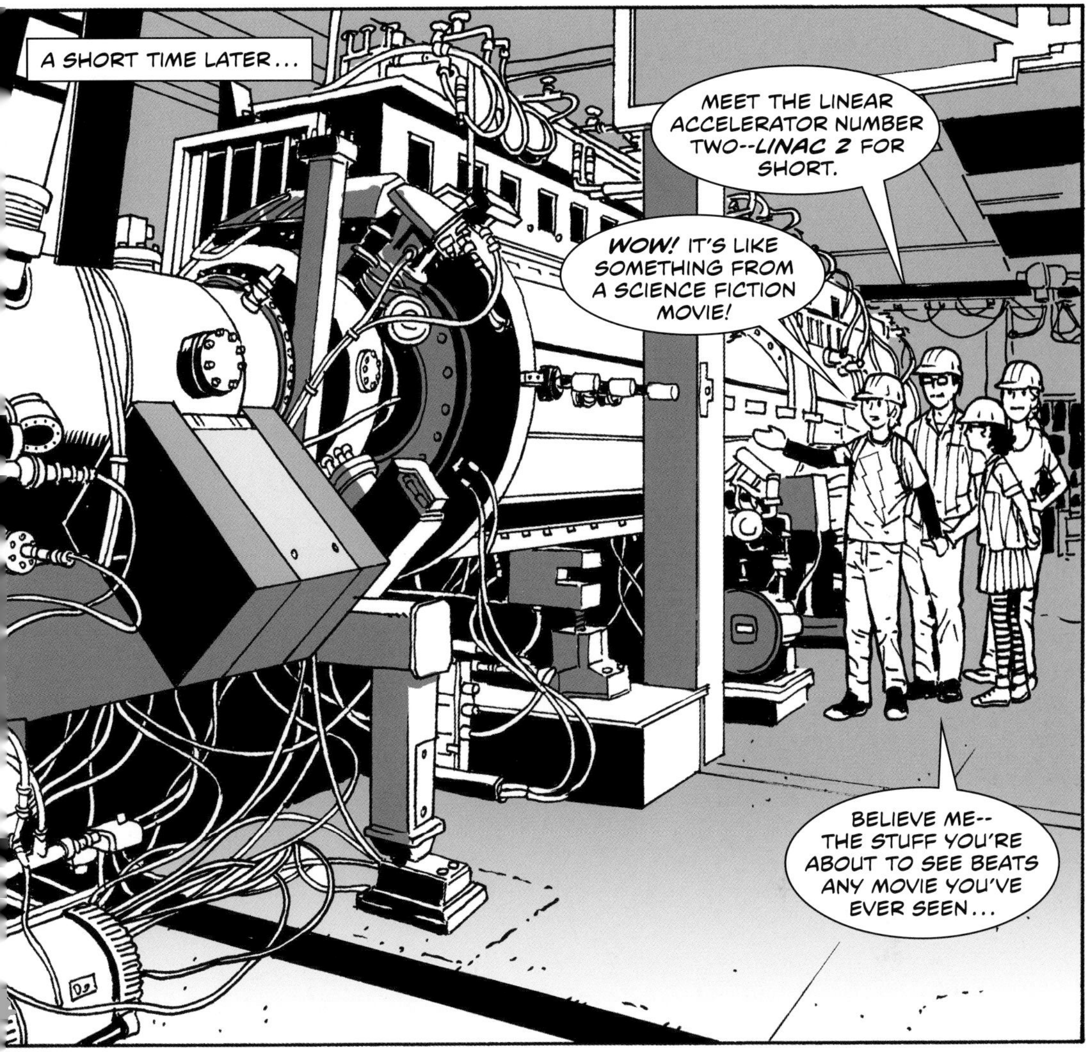
A SHORT TIME LATER...
MEET THE LINEAR ACCELERATOR NUMBER TWO--LINAC 2 FOR SHORT.
WOW! IT'S LIKE SOMETHING FROM A SCIENCE FICTION MOVIE!
BELIEVE ME-- THE STUFF YOU'RE ABOUT TO SEE BEATS ANY MOVIE YOU'VE EVER SEEN...

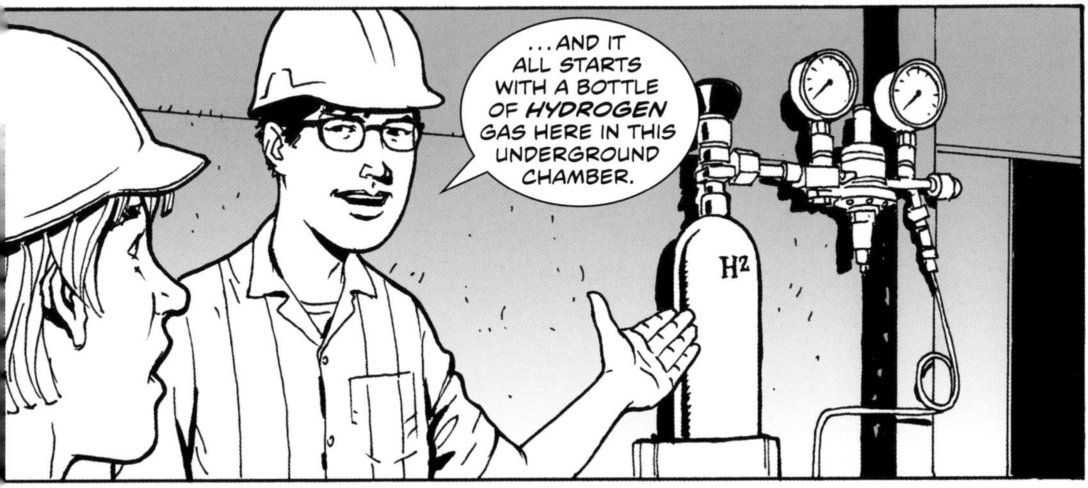
...AND IT ALL STARTS WITH A BOTTLE OF HYDROGEN GAS HERE IN THIS UNDERGROUND CHAMBER.
H2

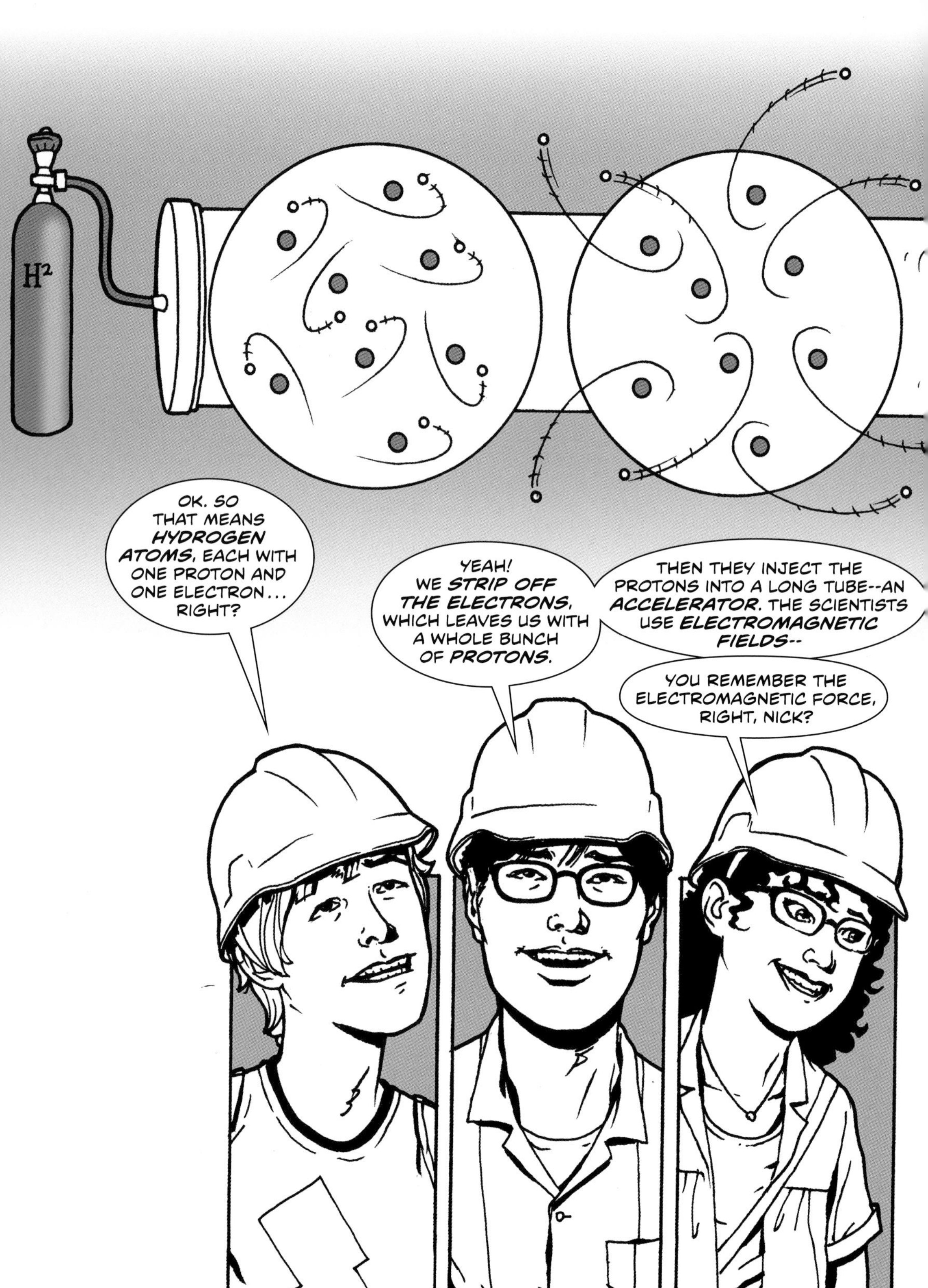

H2
OK. SO THAT MEANS HYDROGEN ATOMS, EACH WITH ONE PROTON AND ONE ELECTRON... RIGHT?
YEAH! WE STRIP OFF THE ELECTRONS, WHICH LEAVES US WITH A WHOLE BUNCH OF PROTONS.
THEN THEY INJECT THE PROTONS INTO A LONG TUBE--AN ACCELERATOR. THE SCIENTISTS USE ELECTROMAGNETIC FIELDS--
YOU REMEMBER THE ELECTROMAGNETIC FORCE, RIGHT, NICK?

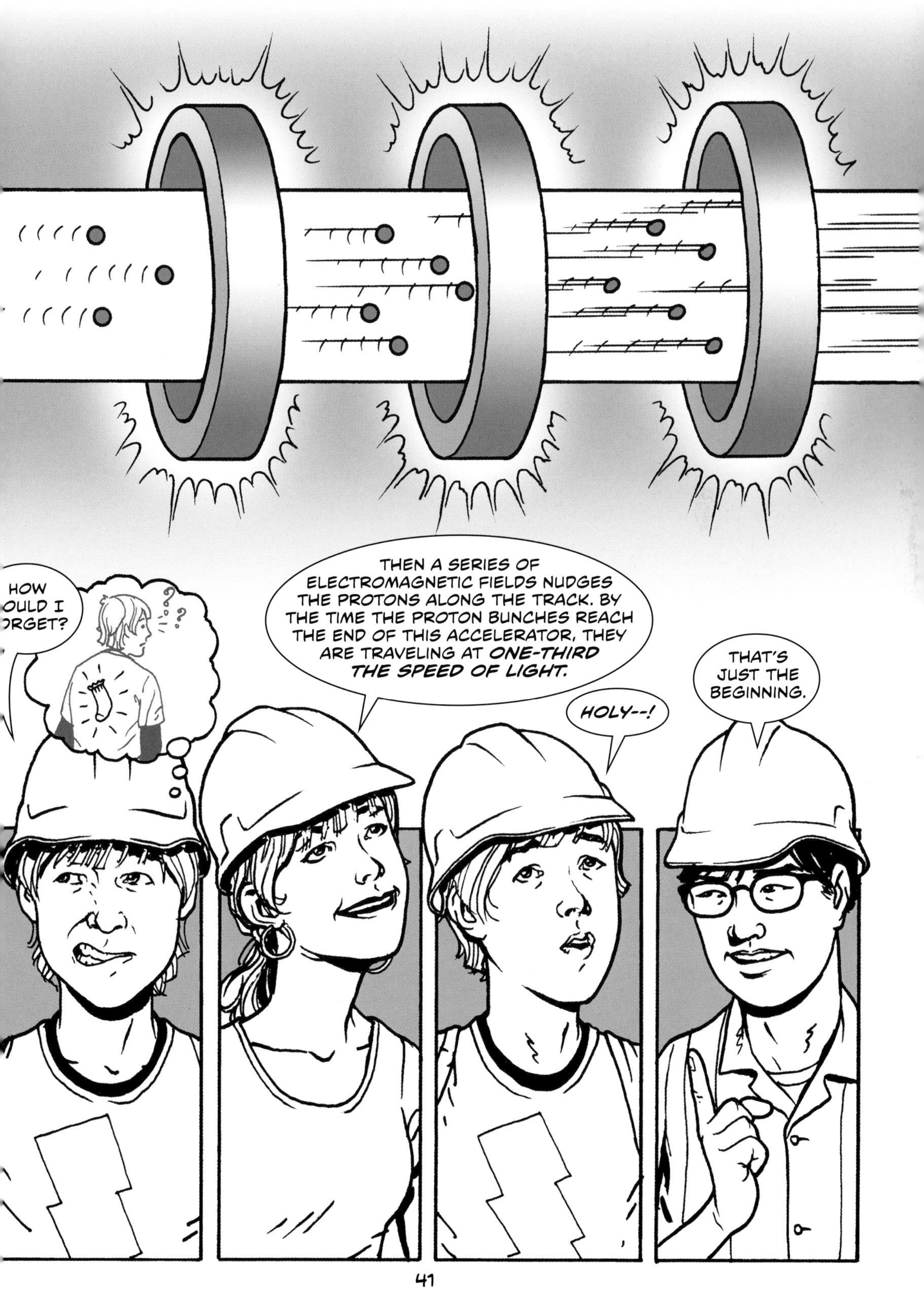
HOW
OULD I
ORGET?
THEN A SERIES OF ELECTROMAGNETIC FIELDS NUDGES THE PROTONS ALONG THE TRACK. BY THE TIME THE PROTON BUNCHES REACH THE END OF THIS ACCELERATOR, THEY ARE TRAVELING AT *ONE-THIRD THE SPEED OF LIGHT.*
HOLY--!
THAT'S JUST THE BEGINNING.

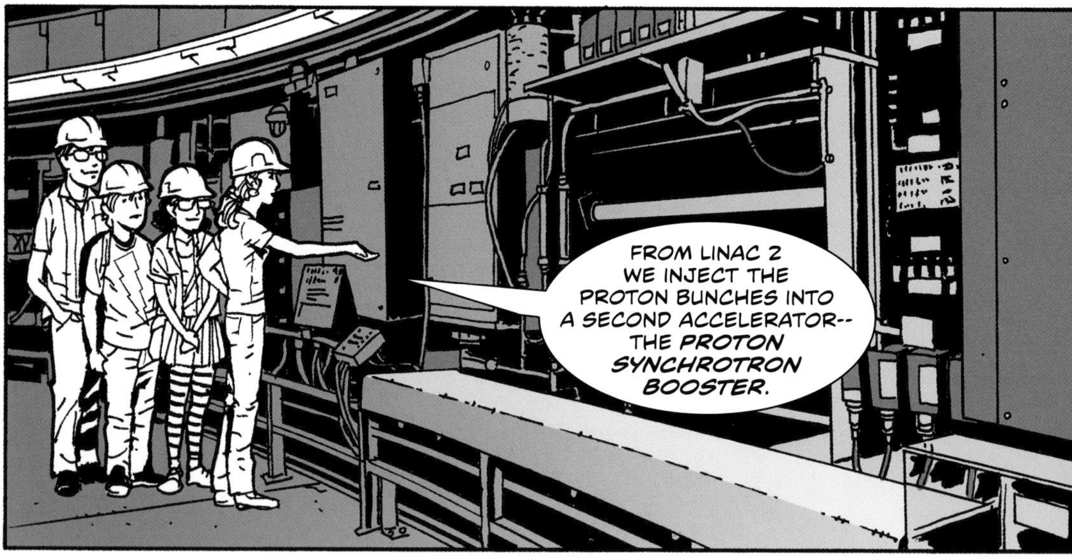
FROM LINAC 2 WE INJECT THE PROTON BUNCHES INTO A SECOND ACCELERATOR-- THE ***PROTON SYNCHROTRON BOOSTER***.

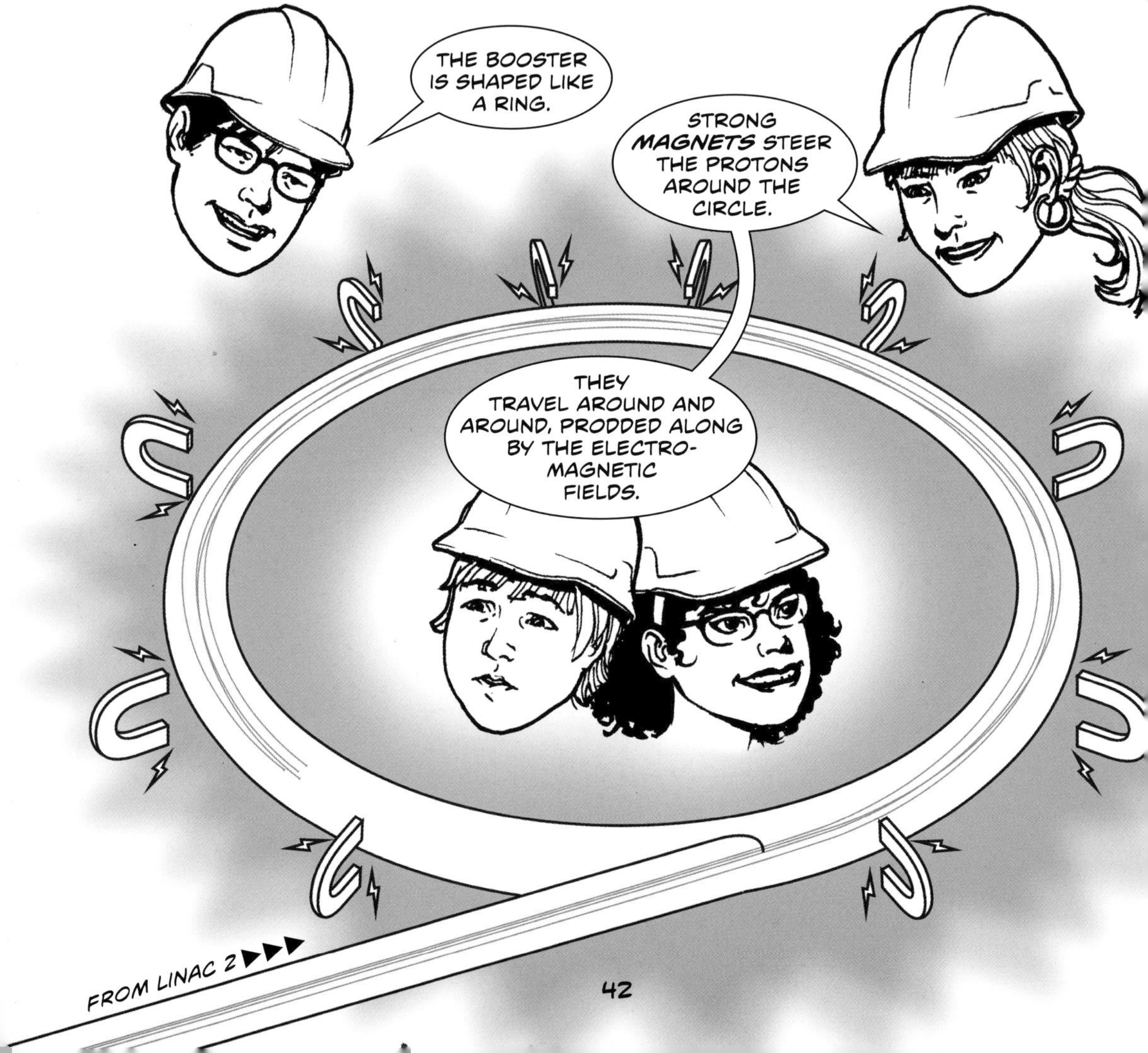
THE BOOSTER IS SHAPED LIKE A RING.
STRONG ***MAGNETS*** STEER THE PROTONS AROUND THE CIRCLE.
THEY TRAVEL AROUND AND AROUND, PRODDED ALONG BY THE ELECTRO-MAGNETIC FIELDS.
FROM LINAC 2 ▶▶▶

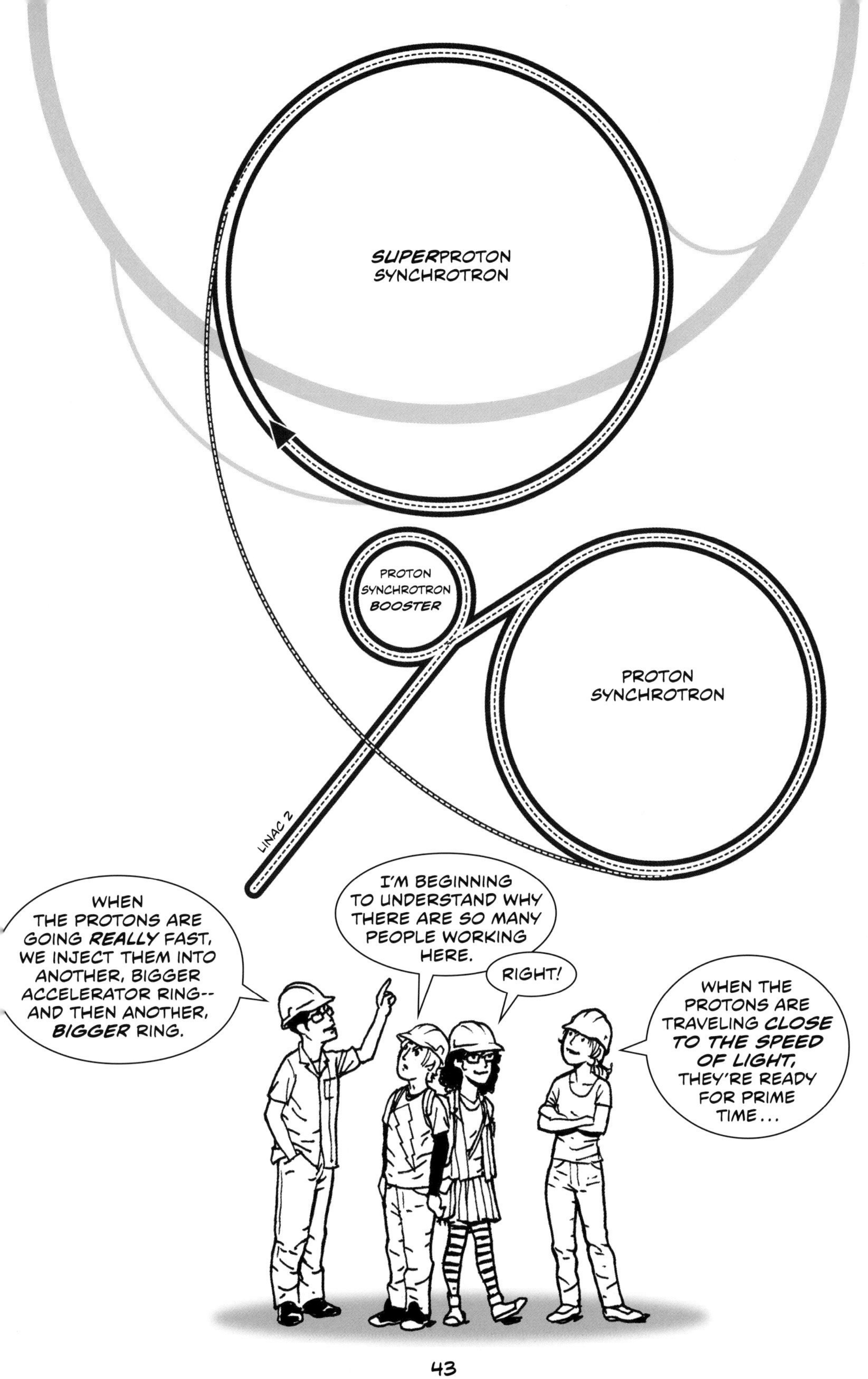
SUPERPROTON SYNCHROTRON
PROTON SYNCHROTRON BOOSTER
PROTON SYNCHROTRON
LINAC 2
WHEN THE PROTONS ARE GOING REALLY FAST, WE INJECT THEM INTO ANOTHER, BIGGER ACCELERATOR RING-- AND THEN ANOTHER, BIGGER RING.
I'M BEGINNING TO UNDERSTAND WHY THERE ARE SO MANY PEOPLE WORKING HERE.
RIGHT!
WHEN THE PROTONS ARE TRAVELING CLOSE TO THE SPEED OF LIGHT, THEY'RE READY FOR PRIME TIME...

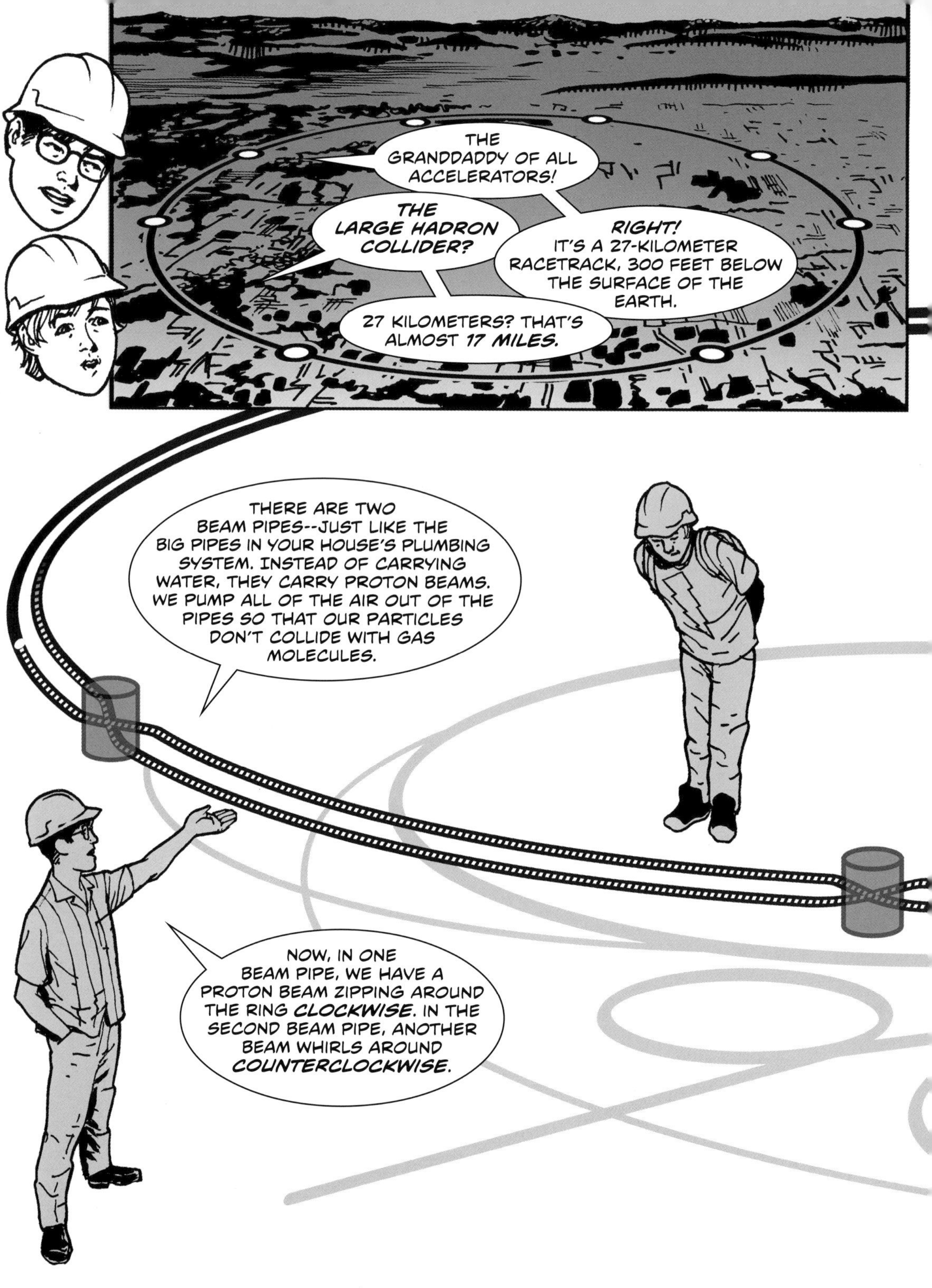
THE GRANDDADDY OF ALL ACCELERATORS!
THE LARGE HADRON COLLIDER?
RIGHT! IT'S A 27-KILOMETER RACETRACK, 300 FEET BELOW THE SURFACE OF THE EARTH.
27 KILOMETERS? THAT'S ALMOST 17 MILES.
THERE ARE TWO BEAM PIPES--JUST LIKE THE BIG PIPES IN YOUR HOUSE'S PLUMBING SYSTEM. INSTEAD OF CARRYING WATER, THEY CARRY PROTON BEAMS. WE PUMP ALL OF THE AIR OUT OF THE PIPES SO THAT OUR PARTICLES DON'T COLLIDE WITH GAS MOLECULES.
NOW, IN ONE BEAM PIPE, WE HAVE A PROTON BEAM ZIPPING AROUND THE RING CLOCKWISE. IN THE SECOND BEAM PIPE, ANOTHER BEAM WHIRLS AROUND COUNTERCLOCKWISE.

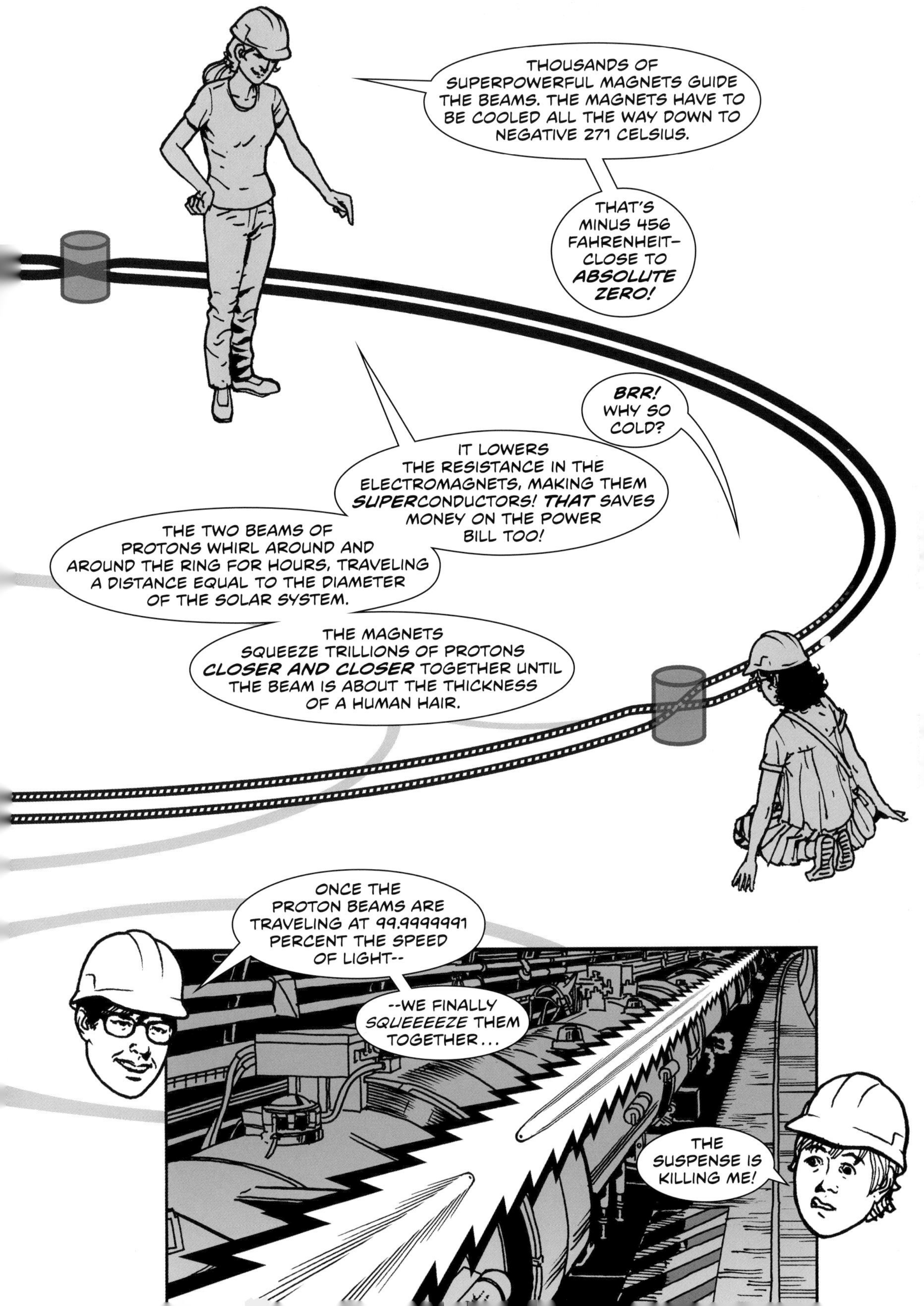

THOUSANDS OF SUPERPOWERFUL MAGNETS GUIDE THE BEAMS. THE MAGNETS HAVE TO BE COOLED ALL THE WAY DOWN TO NEGATIVE 271 CELSIUS.
THAT'S MINUS 456 FAHRENHEIT-CLOSE TO ABSOLUTE ZERO!
BRR! WHY SO COLD?
IT LOWERS THE RESISTANCE IN THE ELECTROMAGNETS, MAKING THEM SUPERCONDUCTORS! THAT SAVES MONEY ON THE POWER BILL TOO!
THE TWO BEAMS OF PROTONS WHIRL AROUND AND AROUND THE RING FOR HOURS, TRAVELING A DISTANCE EQUAL TO THE DIAMETER OF THE SOLAR SYSTEM.
THE MAGNETS SQUEEZE TRILLIONS OF PROTONS CLOSER AND CLOSER TOGETHER UNTIL THE BEAM IS ABOUT THE THICKNESS OF A HUMAN HAIR.
ONCE THE PROTON BEAMS ARE TRAVELING AT 99.9999991 PERCENT THE SPEED OF LIGHT--
--WE FINALLY SQUEEEEEZE THEM TOGETHER...
THE SUSPENSE IS KILLING ME!

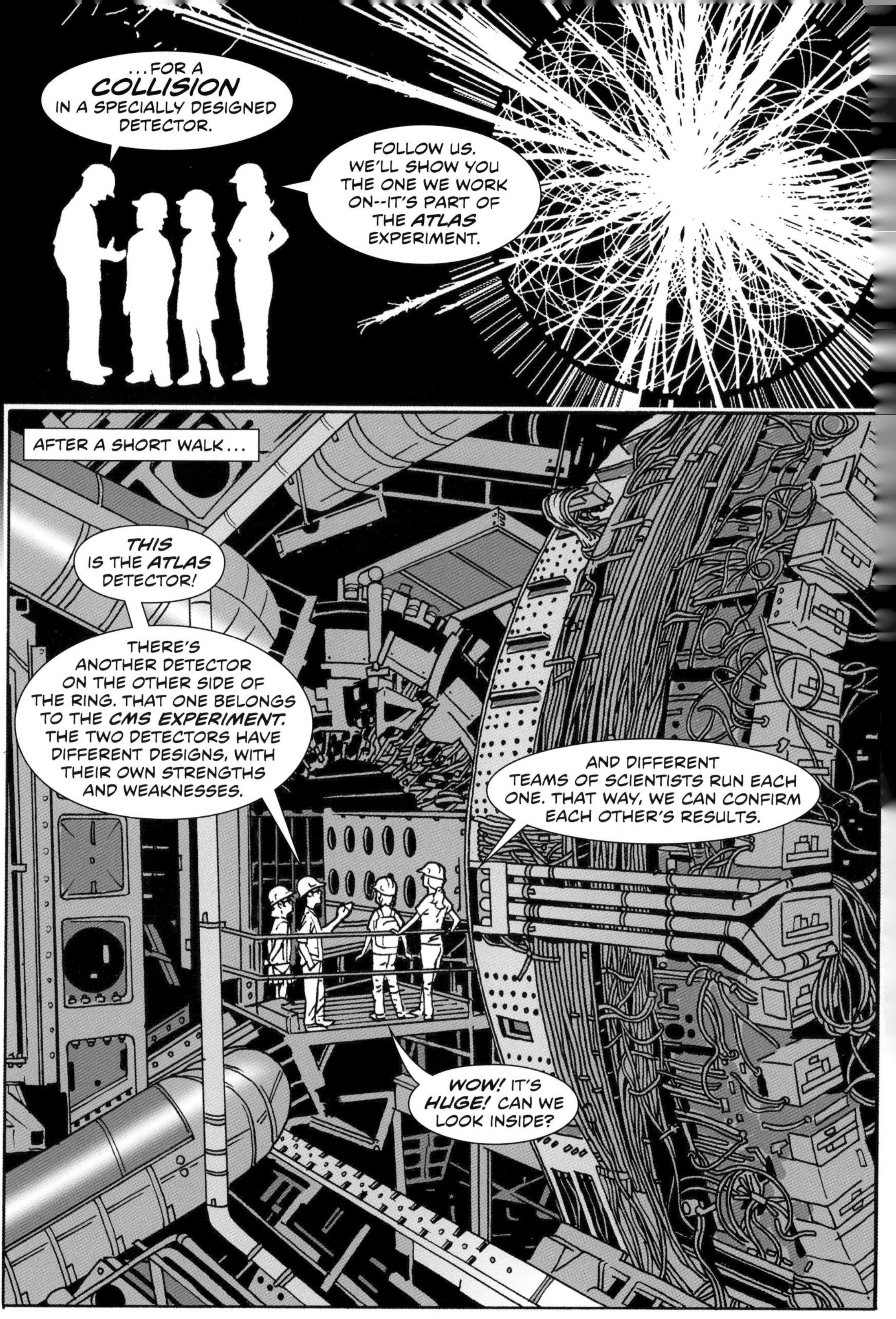
...FOR A COLLISION IN A SPECIALLY DESIGNED DETECTOR.
FOLLOW US. WE'LL SHOW YOU THE ONE WE WORK ON--IT'S PART OF THE ATLAS EXPERIMENT.
AFTER A SHORT WALK...
THIS IS THE ATLAS DETECTOR!
THERE'S ANOTHER DETECTOR ON THE OTHER SIDE OF THE RING. THAT ONE BELONGS TO THE CMS EXPERIMENT. THE TWO DETECTORS HAVE DIFFERENT DESIGNS, WITH THEIR OWN STRENGTHS AND WEAKNESSES.
AND DIFFERENT TEAMS OF SCIENTISTS RUN EACH ONE. THAT WAY, WE CAN CONFIRM EACH OTHER'S RESULTS.
WOW! IT'S HUGE! CAN WE LOOK INSIDE?

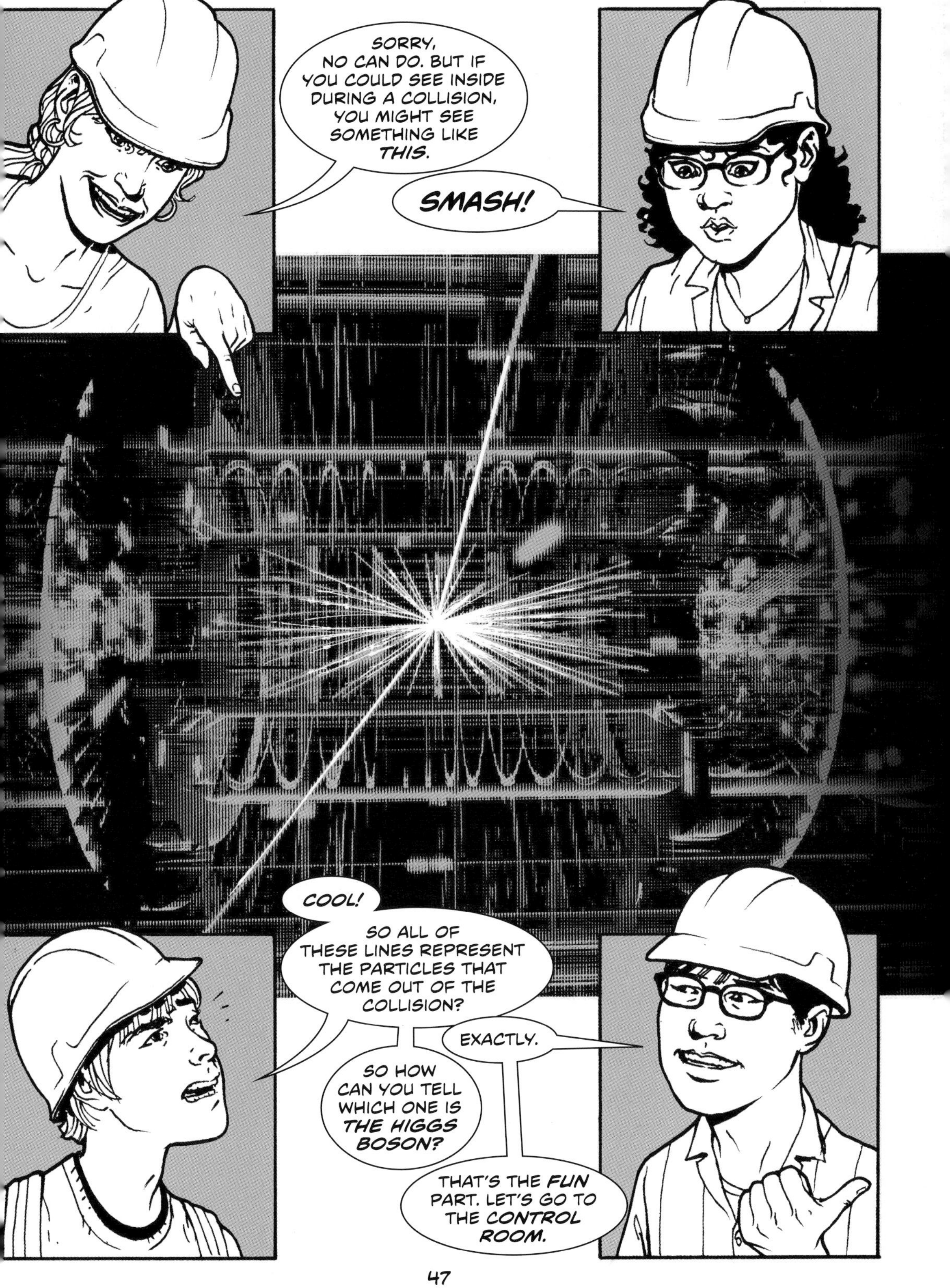

SORRY, NO CAN DO. BUT IF YOU COULD SEE INSIDE DURING A COLLISION, YOU MIGHT SEE SOMETHING LIKE *THIS*.
SMASH!
COOL!
SO ALL OF THESE LINES REPRESENT THE PARTICLES THAT COME OUT OF THE COLLISION?
EXACTLY.
SO HOW CAN YOU TELL WHICH ONE IS ***THE HIGGS BOSON?***
THAT'S THE ***FUN*** PART. LET'S GO TO THE ***CONTROL ROOM.***

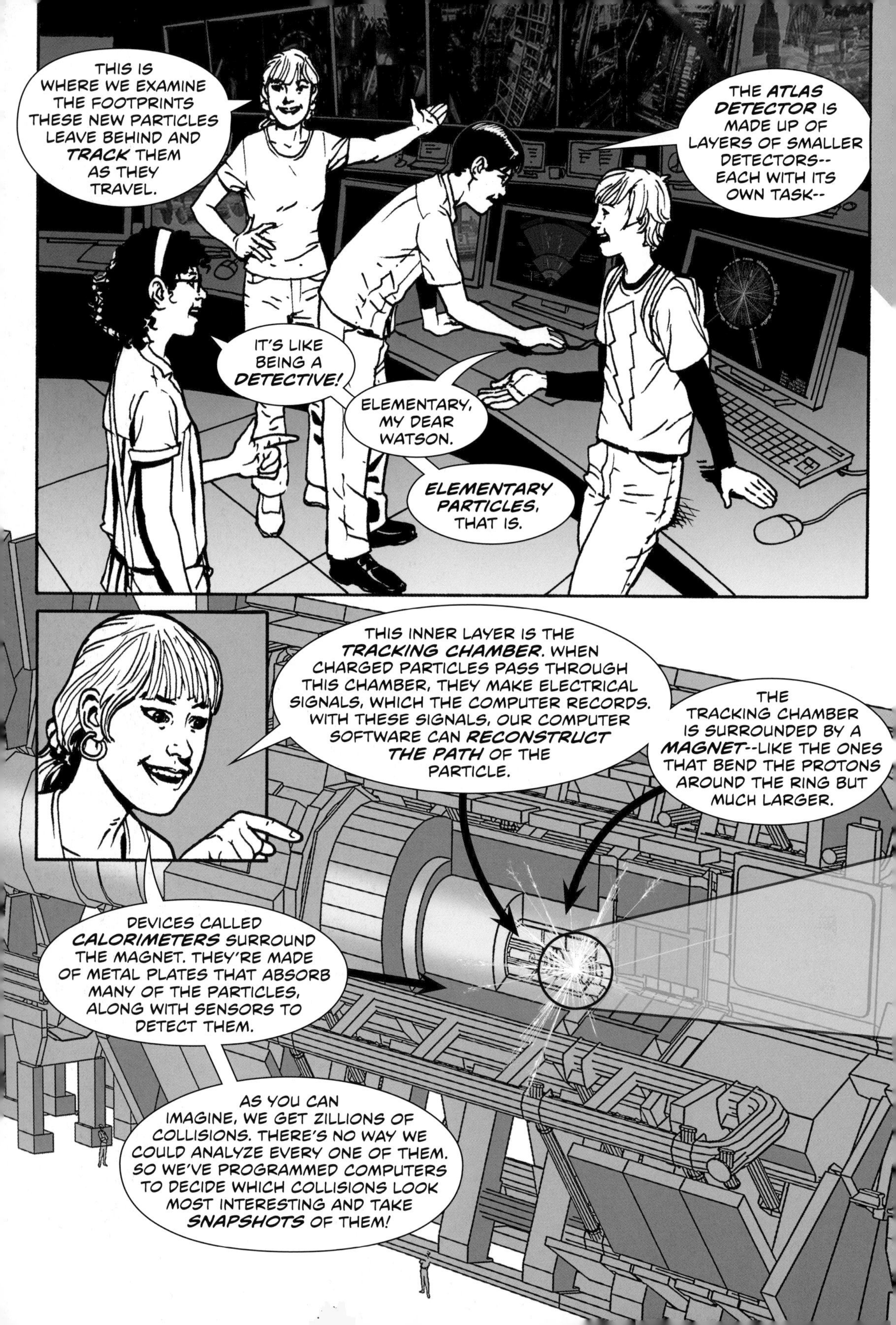
THIS IS WHERE WE EXAMINE THE FOOTPRINTS THESE NEW PARTICLES LEAVE BEHIND AND *TRACK* THEM AS THEY TRAVEL.
THE *ATLAS DETECTOR* IS MADE UP OF LAYERS OF SMALLER DETECTORS--EACH WITH ITS OWN TASK--
IT'S LIKE BEING A *DETECTIVE!*
ELEMENTARY, MY DEAR WATSON.
ELEMENTARY PARTICLES, THAT IS.
THIS INNER LAYER IS THE *TRACKING CHAMBER*. WHEN CHARGED PARTICLES PASS THROUGH THIS CHAMBER, THEY MAKE ELECTRICAL SIGNALS, WHICH THE COMPUTER RECORDS. WITH THESE SIGNALS, OUR COMPUTER SOFTWARE CAN *RECONSTRUCT THE PATH* OF THE PARTICLE.
THE TRACKING CHAMBER IS SURROUNDED BY A *MAGNET*--LIKE THE ONES THAT BEND THE PROTONS AROUND THE RING BUT MUCH LARGER.
DEVICES CALLED *CALORIMETERS* SURROUND THE MAGNET. THEY'RE MADE OF METAL PLATES THAT ABSORB MANY OF THE PARTICLES, ALONG WITH SENSORS TO DETECT THEM.
AS YOU CAN IMAGINE, WE GET ZILLIONS OF COLLISIONS. THERE'S NO WAY WE COULD ANALYZE EVERY ONE OF THEM. SO WE'VE PROGRAMMED COMPUTERS TO DECIDE WHICH COLLISIONS LOOK MOST INTERESTING AND TAKE *SNAPSHOTS* OF THEM!

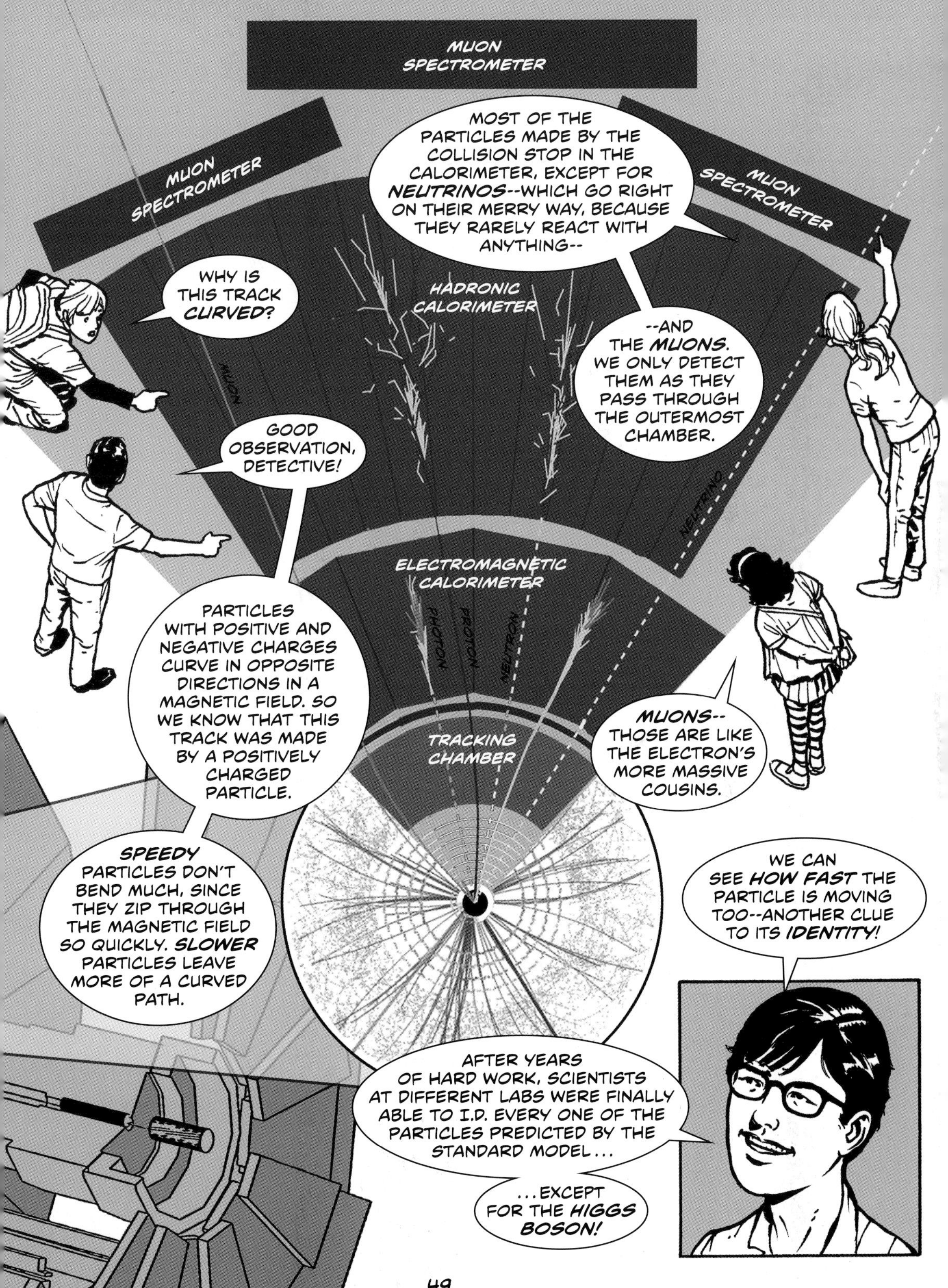
MUON SPECTROMETER
MUON SPECTROMETER
MUON SPECTROMETER
MOST OF THE PARTICLES MADE BY THE COLLISION STOP IN THE CALORIMETER, EXCEPT FOR NEUTRINOS--WHICH GO RIGHT ON THEIR MERRY WAY, BECAUSE THEY RARELY REACT WITH ANYTHING--
WHY IS THIS TRACK CURVED?
HADRONIC CALORIMETER
--AND THE MUONS. WE ONLY DETECT THEM AS THEY PASS THROUGH THE OUTERMOST CHAMBER.
MUON
GOOD OBSERVATION, DETECTIVE!
NEUTRINO
ELECTROMAGNETIC CALORIMETER
PHOTON
PROTON
NEUTRON
PARTICLES WITH POSITIVE AND NEGATIVE CHARGES CURVE IN OPPOSITE DIRECTIONS IN A MAGNETIC FIELD. SO WE KNOW THAT THIS TRACK WAS MADE BY A POSITIVELY CHARGED PARTICLE.
TRACKING CHAMBER
MUONS-- THOSE ARE LIKE THE ELECTRON'S MORE MASSIVE COUSINS.
SPEEDY PARTICLES DON'T BEND MUCH, SINCE THEY ZIP THROUGH THE MAGNETIC FIELD SO QUICKLY. SLOWER PARTICLES LEAVE MORE OF A CURVED PATH.
WE CAN SEE HOW FAST THE PARTICLE IS MOVING TOO--ANOTHER CLUE TO ITS IDENTITY!
AFTER YEARS OF HARD WORK, SCIENTISTS AT DIFFERENT LABS WERE FINALLY ABLE TO I.D. EVERY ONE OF THE PARTICLES PREDICTED BY THE STANDARD MODEL ...
... EXCEPT FOR THE HIGGS BOSON!

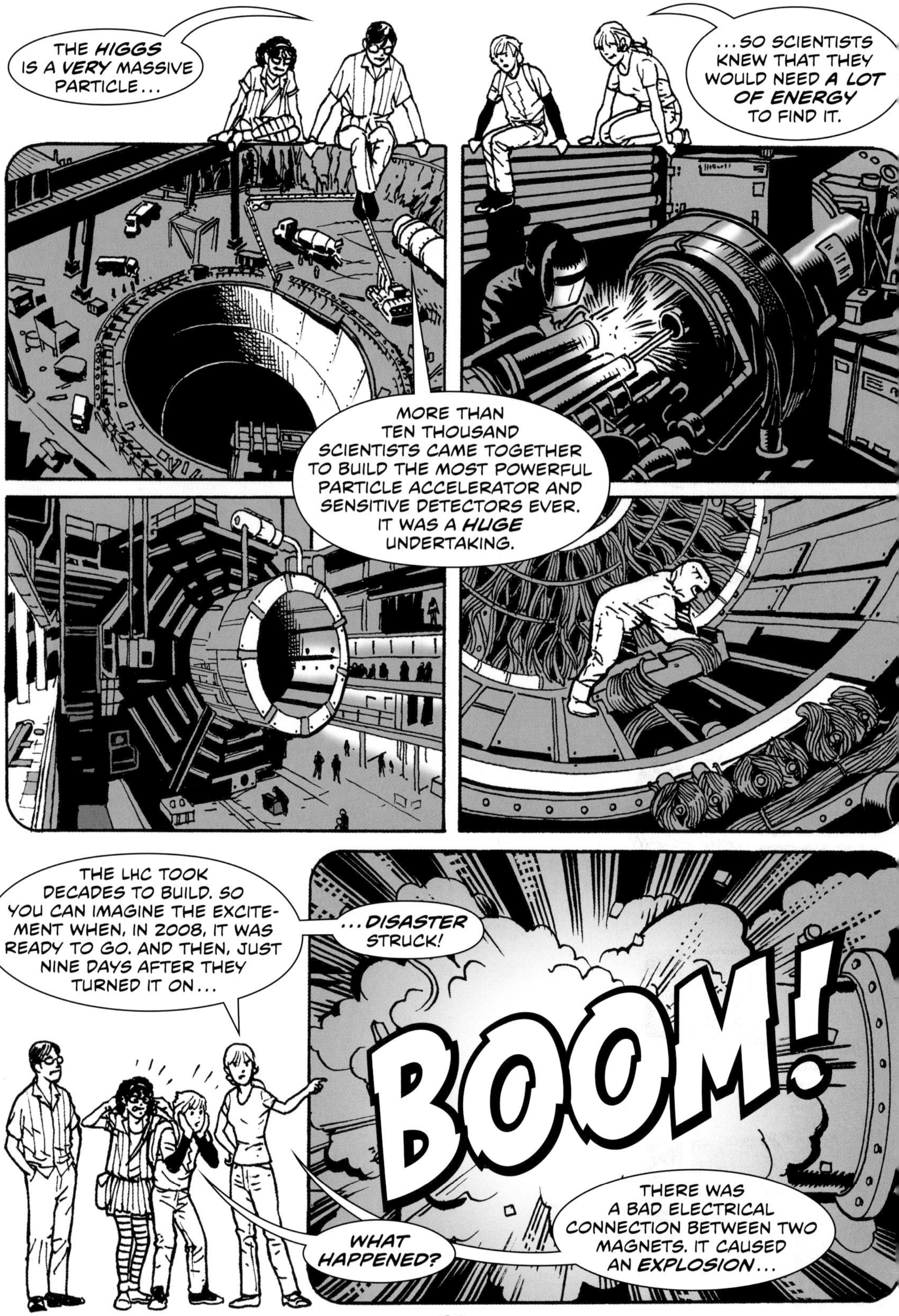
THE *HIGGS* IS A *VERY* MASSIVE PARTICLE...
...SO SCIENTISTS KNEW THAT THEY WOULD NEED *A LOT OF ENERGY* TO FIND IT.
MORE THAN TEN THOUSAND SCIENTISTS CAME TOGETHER TO BUILD THE MOST POWERFUL PARTICLE ACCELERATOR AND SENSITIVE DETECTORS EVER. IT WAS A *HUGE* UNDERTAKING.
THE LHC TOOK DECADES TO BUILD. SO YOU CAN IMAGINE THE EXCITEMENT WHEN, IN 2008, IT WAS READY TO GO. AND THEN, JUST NINE DAYS AFTER THEY TURNED IT ON...
...*DISASTER* STRUCK!
BOOM!
WHAT HAPPENED?
THERE WAS A BAD ELECTRICAL CONNECTION BETWEEN TWO MAGNETS. IT CAUSED AN *EXPLOSION*...

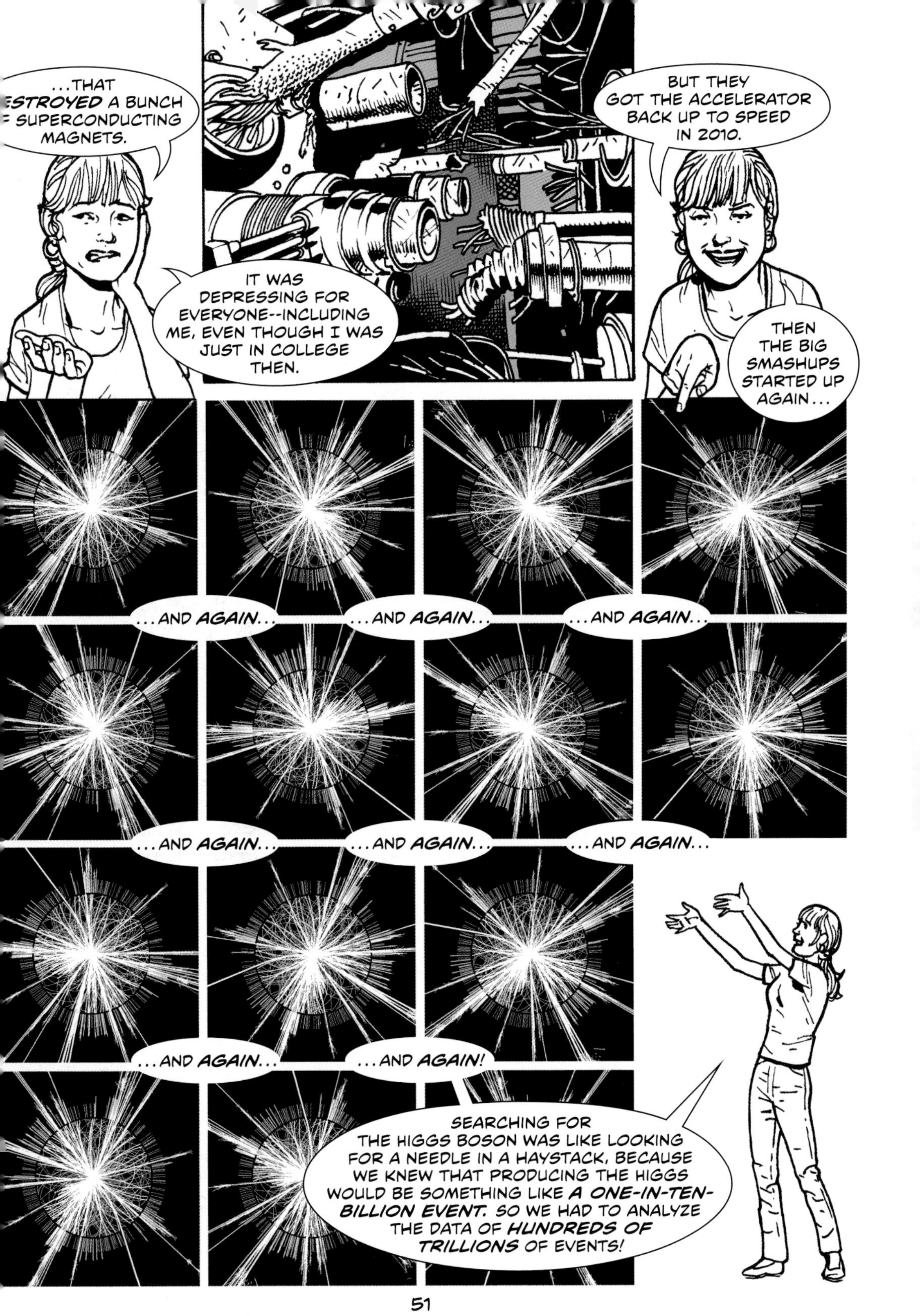
...THAT
ESTROYED A BUNCH
F SUPERCONDUCTING
MAGNETS.
IT WAS DEPRESSING FOR EVERYONE--INCLUDING ME, EVEN THOUGH I WAS JUST IN COLLEGE THEN.
BUT THEY GOT THE ACCELERATOR BACK UP TO SPEED IN 2010.
THEN THE BIG SMASHUPS STARTED UP AGAIN...
...AND AGAIN...
...AND AGAIN...
...AND AGAIN...
...AND AGAIN...
...AND AGAIN...
...AND AGAIN...
...AND AGAIN...
...AND AGAIN!
SEARCHING FOR THE HIGGS BOSON WAS LIKE LOOKING FOR A NEEDLE IN A HAYSTACK, BECAUSE WE KNEW THAT PRODUCING THE HIGGS WOULD BE SOMETHING LIKE A ONE-IN-TEN-BILLION EVENT. SO WE HAD TO ANALYZE THE DATA OF HUNDREDS OF TRILLIONS OF EVENTS!

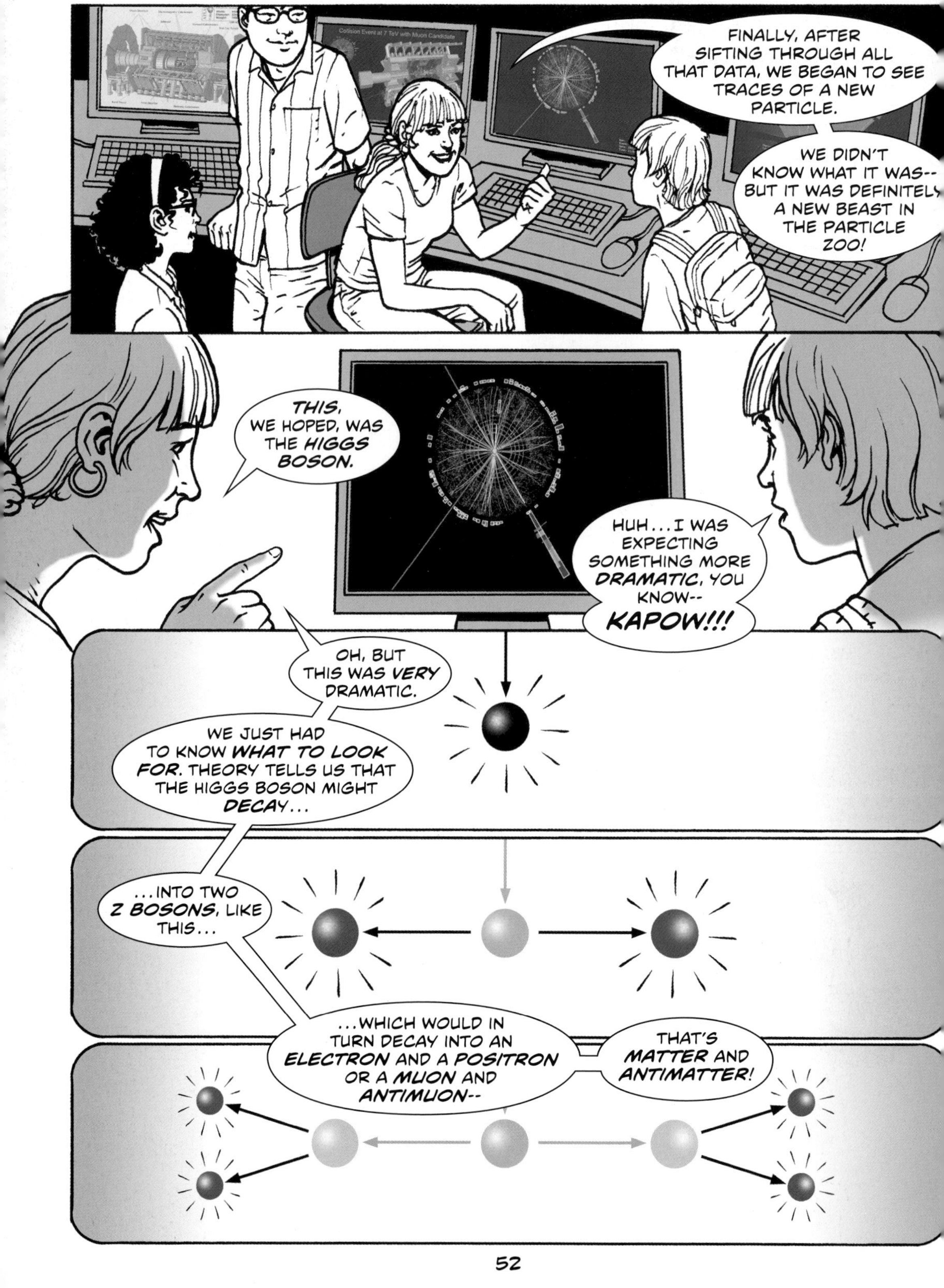
FINALLY, AFTER SIFTING THROUGH ALL THAT DATA, WE BEGAN TO SEE TRACES OF A NEW PARTICLE.
WE DIDN'T KNOW WHAT IT WAS-- BUT IT WAS DEFINITELY A NEW BEAST IN THE PARTICLE ZOO!
THIS, WE HOPED, WAS THE *HIGGS BOSON*.
HUH . . . I WAS EXPECTING SOMETHING MORE *DRAMATIC*, YOU KNOW--
KAPOW!!!
OH, BUT THIS WAS *VERY* DRAMATIC.
WE JUST HAD TO KNOW *WHAT TO LOOK FOR*. THEORY TELLS US THAT THE HIGGS BOSON MIGHT *DECAY*...
...INTO TWO *Z BOSONS*, LIKE THIS...
...WHICH WOULD IN TURN DECAY INTO AN *ELECTRON* AND A *POSITRON* OR A *MUON* AND *ANTIMUON*--
THAT'S *MATTER* AND *ANTIMATTER*!

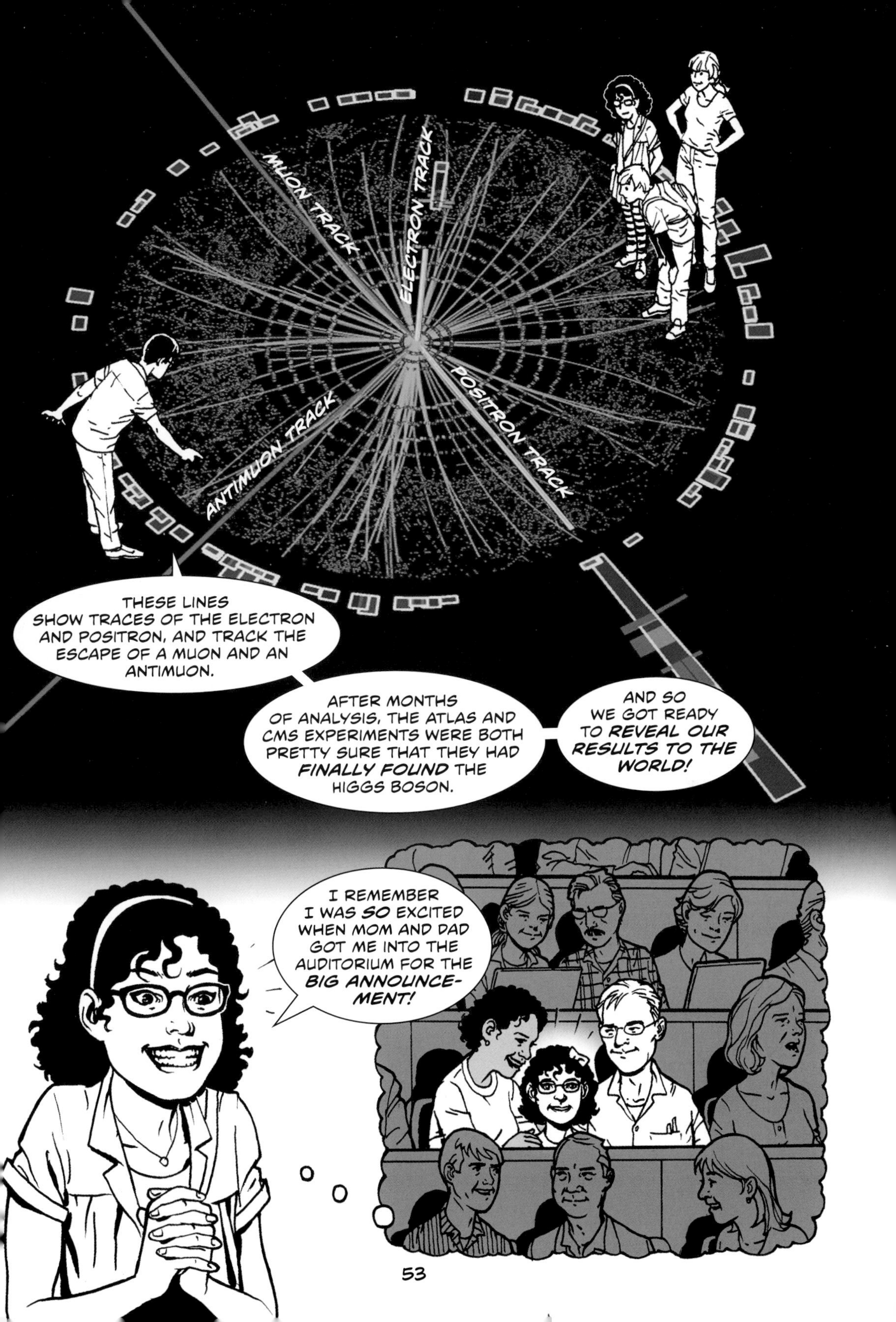
MUON TRACK
ELECTRON TRACK
ANTIMUON TRACK
POSITRON TRACK
THESE LINES SHOW TRACES OF THE ELECTRON AND POSITRON, AND TRACK THE ESCAPE OF A MUON AND AN ANTIMUON.
AFTER MONTHS OF ANALYSIS, THE ATLAS AND CMS EXPERIMENTS WERE BOTH PRETTY SURE THAT THEY HAD ***FINALLY FOUND*** THE HIGGS BOSON.
AND SO WE GOT READY TO ***REVEAL OUR RESULTS TO THE WORLD!***
I REMEMBER I WAS ***SO*** EXCITED WHEN MOM AND DAD GOT ME INTO THE AUDITORIUM FOR THE ***BIG ANNOUNCE-MENT!***

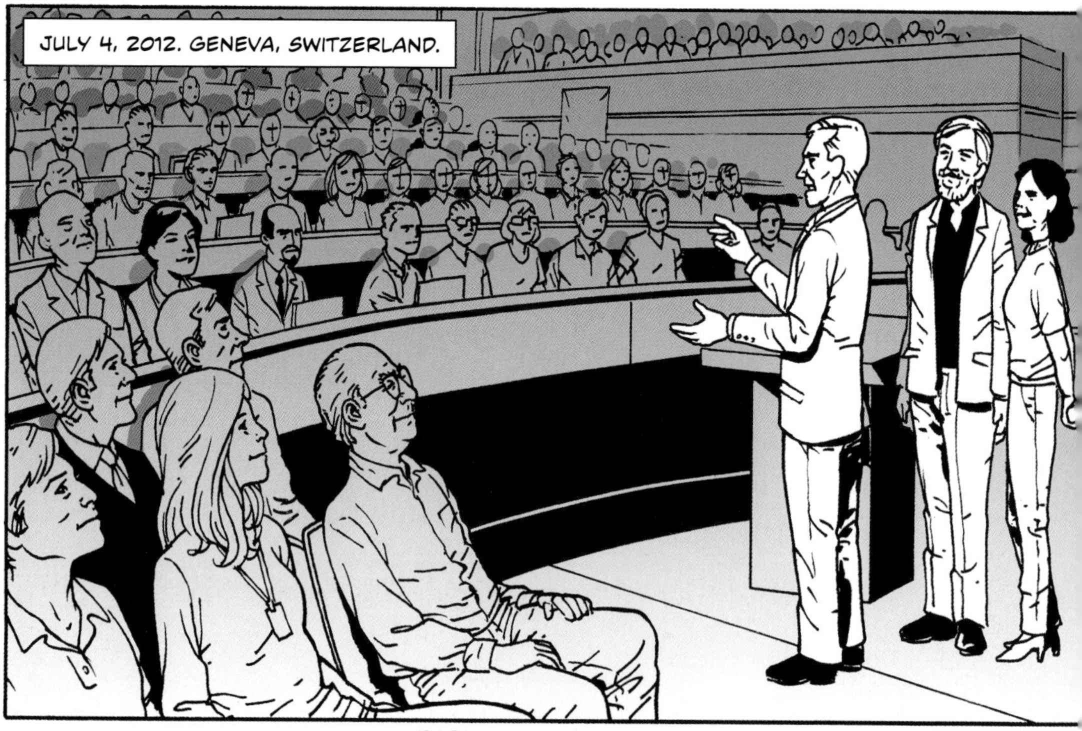
JULY 4, 2012. GENEVA, SWITZERLAND.

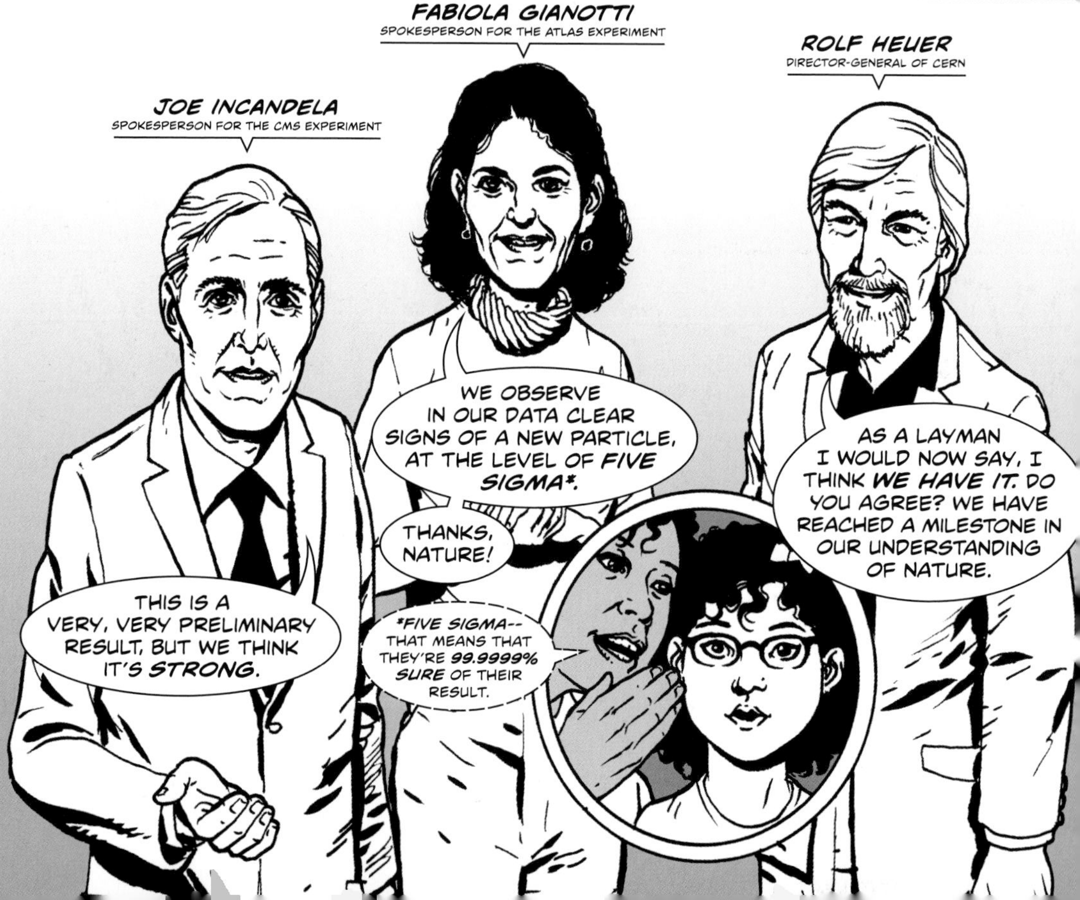
FABIOLA GIANOTTI
SPOKESPERSON FOR THE ATLAS EXPERIMENT
ROLF HEUER
DIRECTOR-GENERAL OF CERN
JOE INCANDELA
SPOKESPERSON FOR THE CMS EXPERIMENT
THIS IS A VERY, VERY PRELIMINARY RESULT, BUT WE THINK IT'S STRONG.
WE OBSERVE IN OUR DATA CLEAR SIGNS OF A NEW PARTICLE, AT THE LEVEL OF FIVE SIGMA*.
THANKS, NATURE!
*FIVE SIGMA-- THAT MEANS THAT THEY'RE 99.9999% SURE OF THEIR RESULT.
AS A LAYMAN I WOULD NOW SAY, I THINK WE HAVE IT. DO YOU AGREE? WE HAVE REACHED A MILESTONE IN OUR UNDERSTANDING OF NATURE.

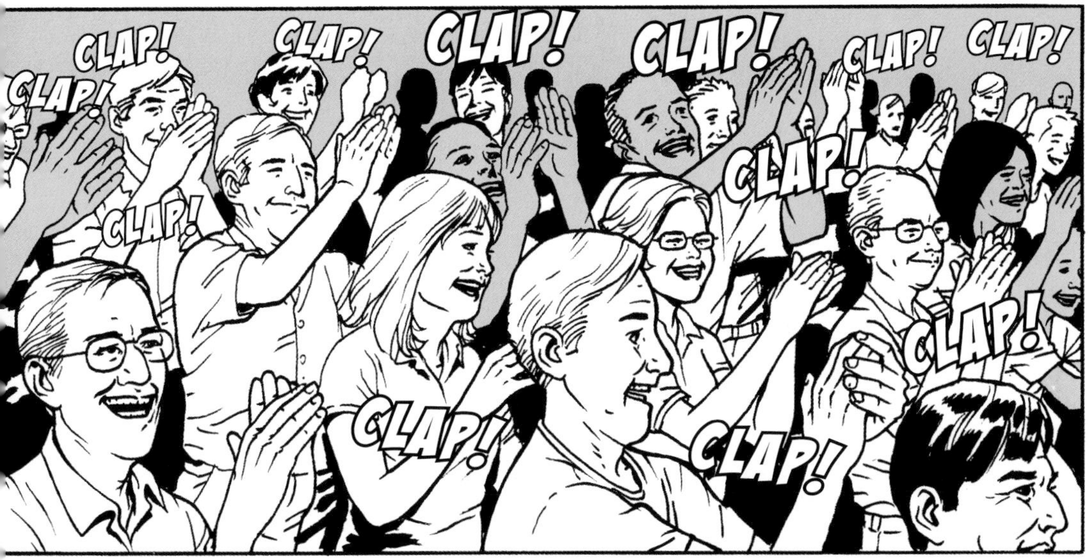
CLAP!
CLAP!
CLAP!
CLAP!
CLAP!
CLAP!
CLAP!
CLAP!
CLAP!
CLAP!
CLAP!
CLAP!

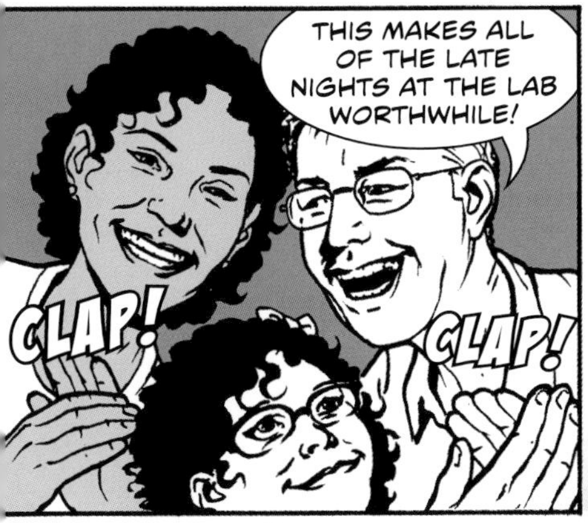
THIS MAKES ALL OF THE LATE NIGHTS AT THE LAB WORTHWHILE!
CLAP!
CLAP!

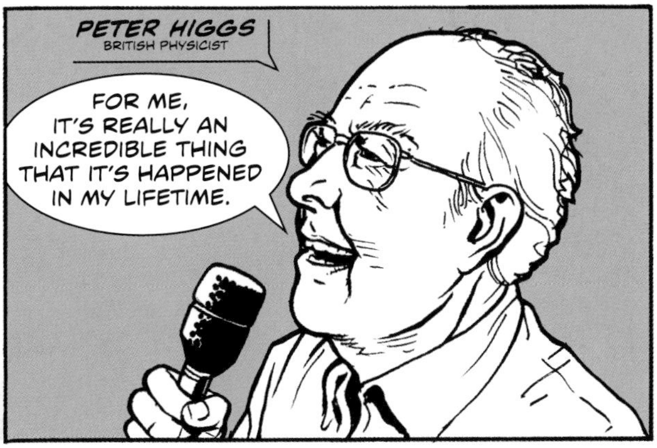
PETER HIGGS
BRITISH PHYSICIST
FOR ME, IT'S REALLY AN INCREDIBLE THING THAT IT'S HAPPENED IN MY LIFETIME.

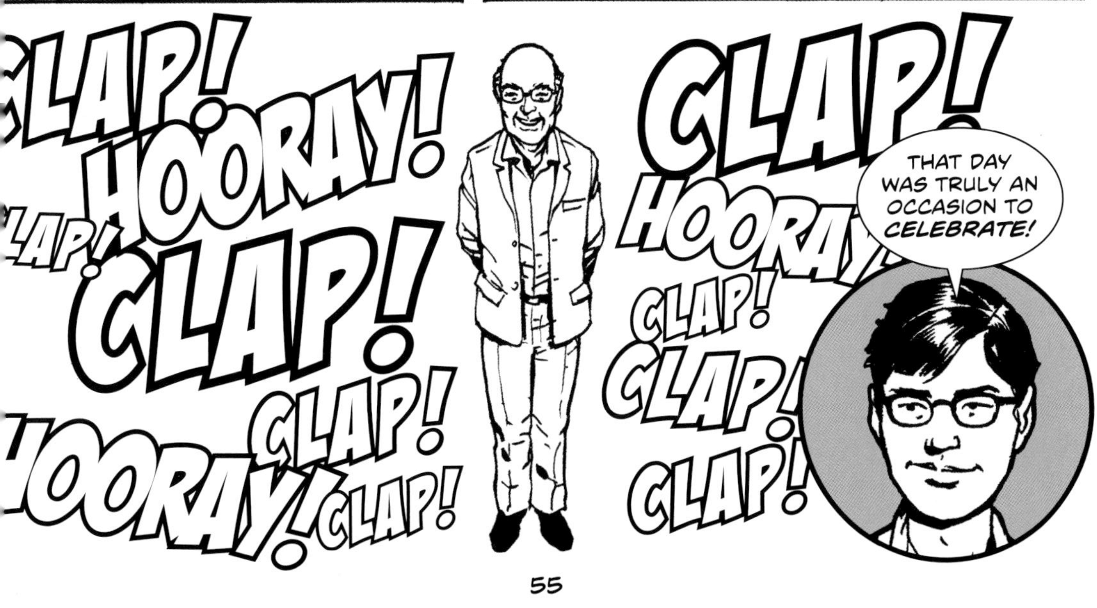
CLAP!
HOORAY!
CLAP!
CLAP!
CLAP!
HOORAY!
CLAP!
CLAP!
HOORAY!
CLAP!
CLAP!
CLAP!
THAT DAY WAS TRULY AN OCCASION TO *CELEBRATE!*

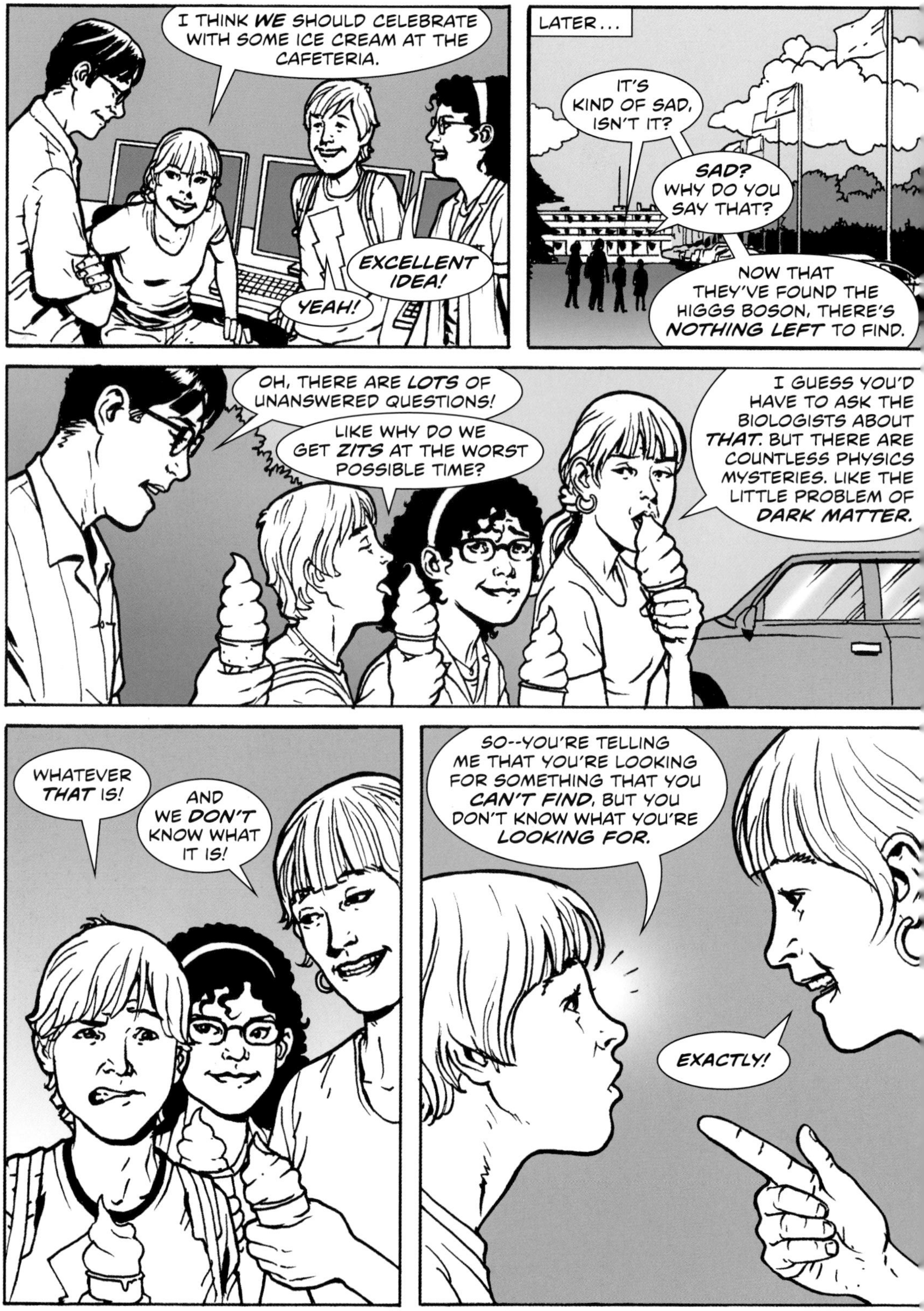
I THINK WE SHOULD CELEBRATE WITH SOME ICE CREAM AT THE CAFETERIA.
YEAH!
EXCELLENT IDEA!
LATER...
IT'S KIND OF SAD, ISN'T IT?
SAD? WHY DO YOU SAY THAT?
NOW THAT THEY'VE FOUND THE HIGGS BOSON, THERE'S NOTHING LEFT TO FIND.
OH, THERE ARE LOTS OF UNANSWERED QUESTIONS!
LIKE WHY DO WE GET ZITS AT THE WORST POSSIBLE TIME?
I GUESS YOU'D HAVE TO ASK THE BIOLOGISTS ABOUT THAT. BUT THERE ARE COUNTLESS PHYSICS MYSTERIES. LIKE THE LITTLE PROBLEM OF DARK MATTER.
WHATEVER THAT IS!
AND WE DON'T KNOW WHAT IT IS!
SO--YOU'RE TELLING ME THAT YOU'RE LOOKING FOR SOMETHING THAT YOU CAN'T FIND, BUT YOU DON'T KNOW WHAT YOU'RE LOOKING FOR.
EXACTLY!

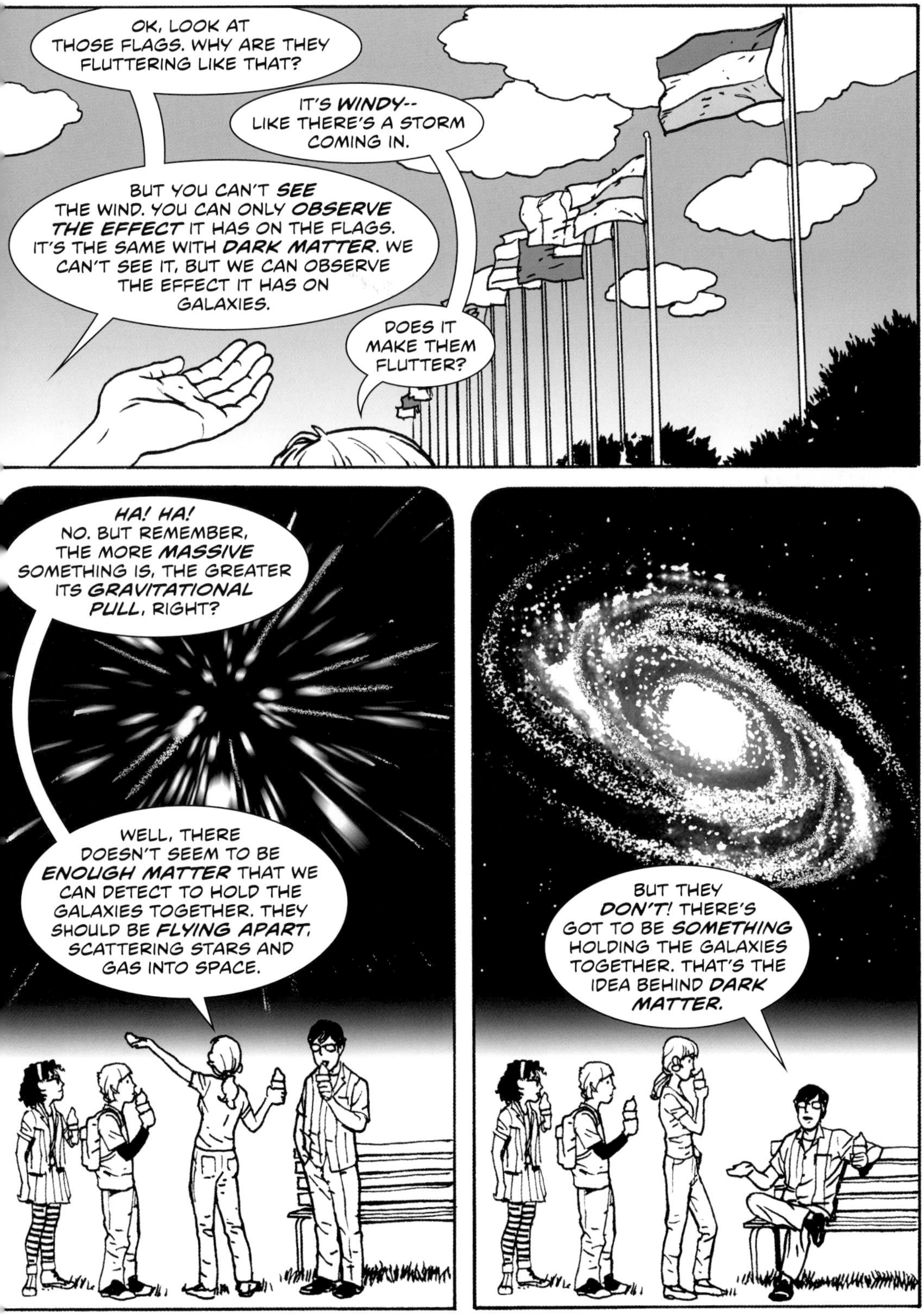
OK, LOOK AT THOSE FLAGS. WHY ARE THEY FLUTTERING LIKE THAT?
IT'S WINDY-- LIKE THERE'S A STORM COMING IN.
BUT YOU CAN'T SEE THE WIND. YOU CAN ONLY OBSERVE THE EFFECT IT HAS ON THE FLAGS. IT'S THE SAME WITH DARK MATTER. WE CAN'T SEE IT, BUT WE CAN OBSERVE THE EFFECT IT HAS ON GALAXIES.
DOES IT MAKE THEM FLUTTER?
HA! HA! NO. BUT REMEMBER, THE MORE MASSIVE SOMETHING IS, THE GREATER ITS GRAVITATIONAL PULL, RIGHT?
WELL, THERE DOESN'T SEEM TO BE ENOUGH MATTER THAT WE CAN DETECT TO HOLD THE GALAXIES TOGETHER. THEY SHOULD BE FLYING APART, SCATTERING STARS AND GAS INTO SPACE.
BUT THEY DON'T! THERE'S GOT TO BE SOMETHING HOLDING THE GALAXIES TOGETHER. THAT'S THE IDEA BEHIND DARK MATTER.

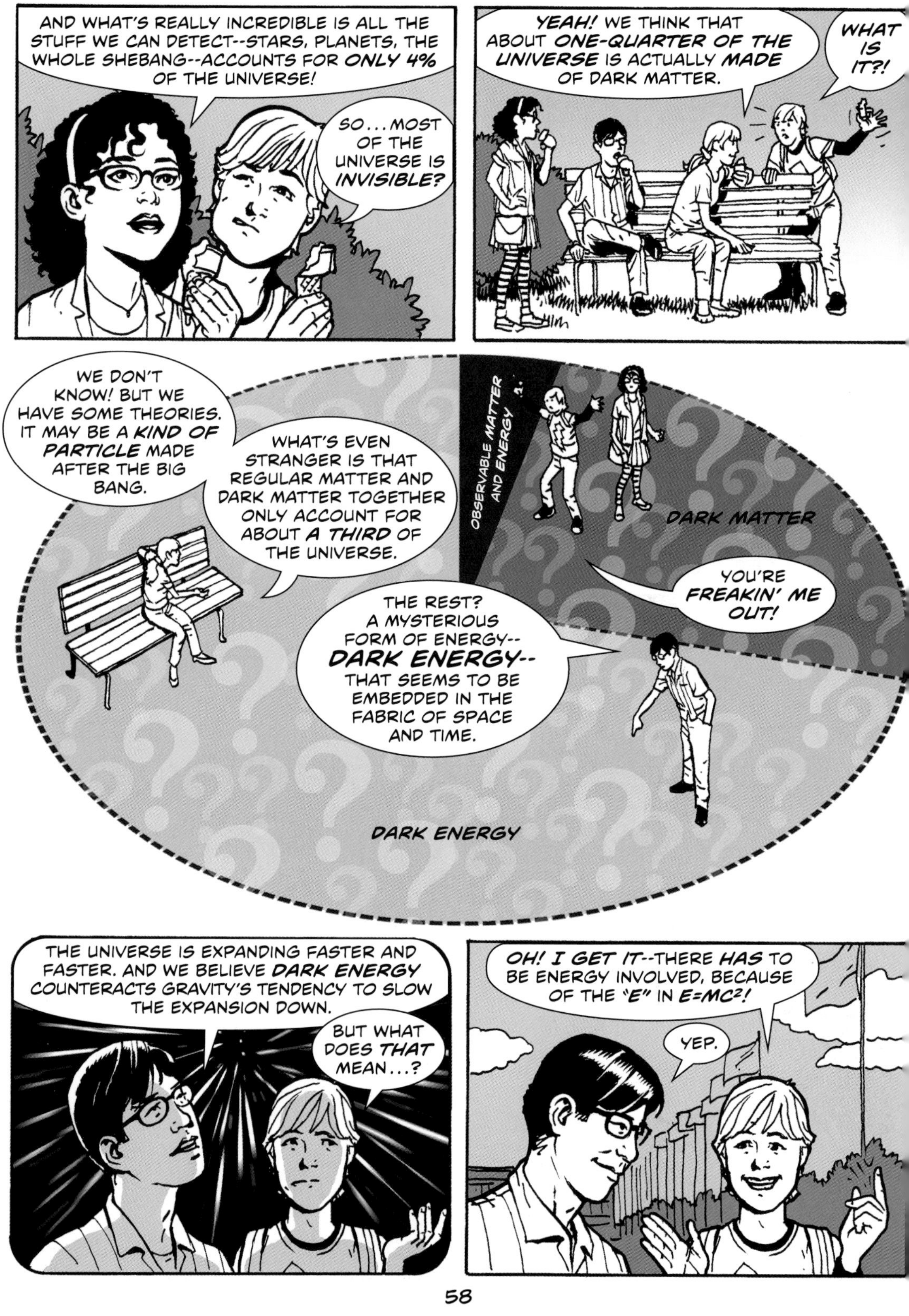

AND WHAT'S REALLY INCREDIBLE IS ALL THE STUFF WE CAN DETECT--STARS, PLANETS, THE WHOLE SHEBANG--ACCOUNTS FOR ONLY 4% OF THE UNIVERSE!
SO... MOST OF THE UNIVERSE IS INVISIBLE?
YEAH! WE THINK THAT ABOUT ONE-QUARTER OF THE UNIVERSE IS ACTUALLY MADE OF DARK MATTER.
WHAT IS IT?!
WE DON'T KNOW! BUT WE HAVE SOME THEORIES. IT MAY BE A KIND OF PARTICLE MADE AFTER THE BIG BANG.
WHAT'S EVEN STRANGER IS THAT REGULAR MATTER AND DARK MATTER TOGETHER ONLY ACCOUNT FOR ABOUT A THIRD OF THE UNIVERSE.
OBSERVABLE MATTER AND ENERGY
DARK MATTER
YOU'RE FREAKIN' ME OUT!
THE REST? A MYSTERIOUS FORM OF ENERGY-- DARK ENERGY-- THAT SEEMS TO BE EMBEDDED IN THE FABRIC OF SPACE AND TIME.
DARK ENERGY
THE UNIVERSE IS EXPANDING FASTER AND FASTER. AND WE BELIEVE DARK ENERGY COUNTERACTS GRAVITY'S TENDENCY TO SLOW THE EXPANSION DOWN.
BUT WHAT DOES THAT MEAN...?
OH! I GET IT--THERE HAS TO BE ENERGY INVOLVED, BECAUSE OF THE "E" IN E=MC²!
YEP.

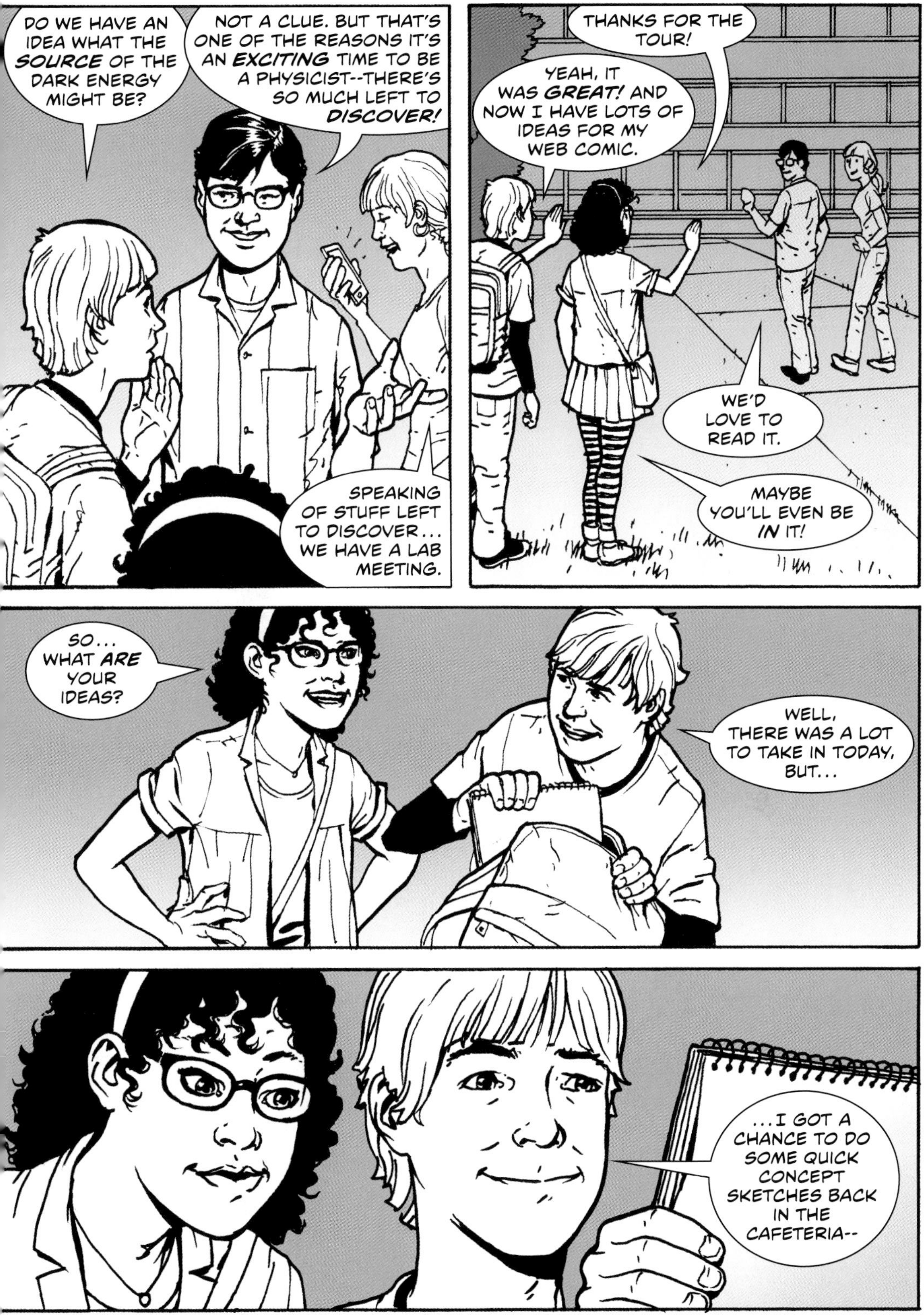
DO WE HAVE AN IDEA WHAT THE SOURCE OF THE DARK ENERGY MIGHT BE?
NOT A CLUE. BUT THAT'S ONE OF THE REASONS IT'S AN EXCITING TIME TO BE A PHYSICIST--THERE'S SO MUCH LEFT TO DISCOVER!
SPEAKING OF STUFF LEFT TO DISCOVER... WE HAVE A LAB MEETING.
THANKS FOR THE TOUR!
YEAH, IT WAS GREAT! AND NOW I HAVE LOTS OF IDEAS FOR MY WEB COMIC.
WE'D LOVE TO READ IT.
MAYBE YOU'LL EVEN BE IN IT!
SO... WHAT ARE YOUR IDEAS?
WELL, THERE WAS A LOT TO TAKE IN TODAY, BUT...
...I GOT A CHANCE TO DO SOME QUICK CONCEPT SKETCHES BACK IN THE CAFETERIA--

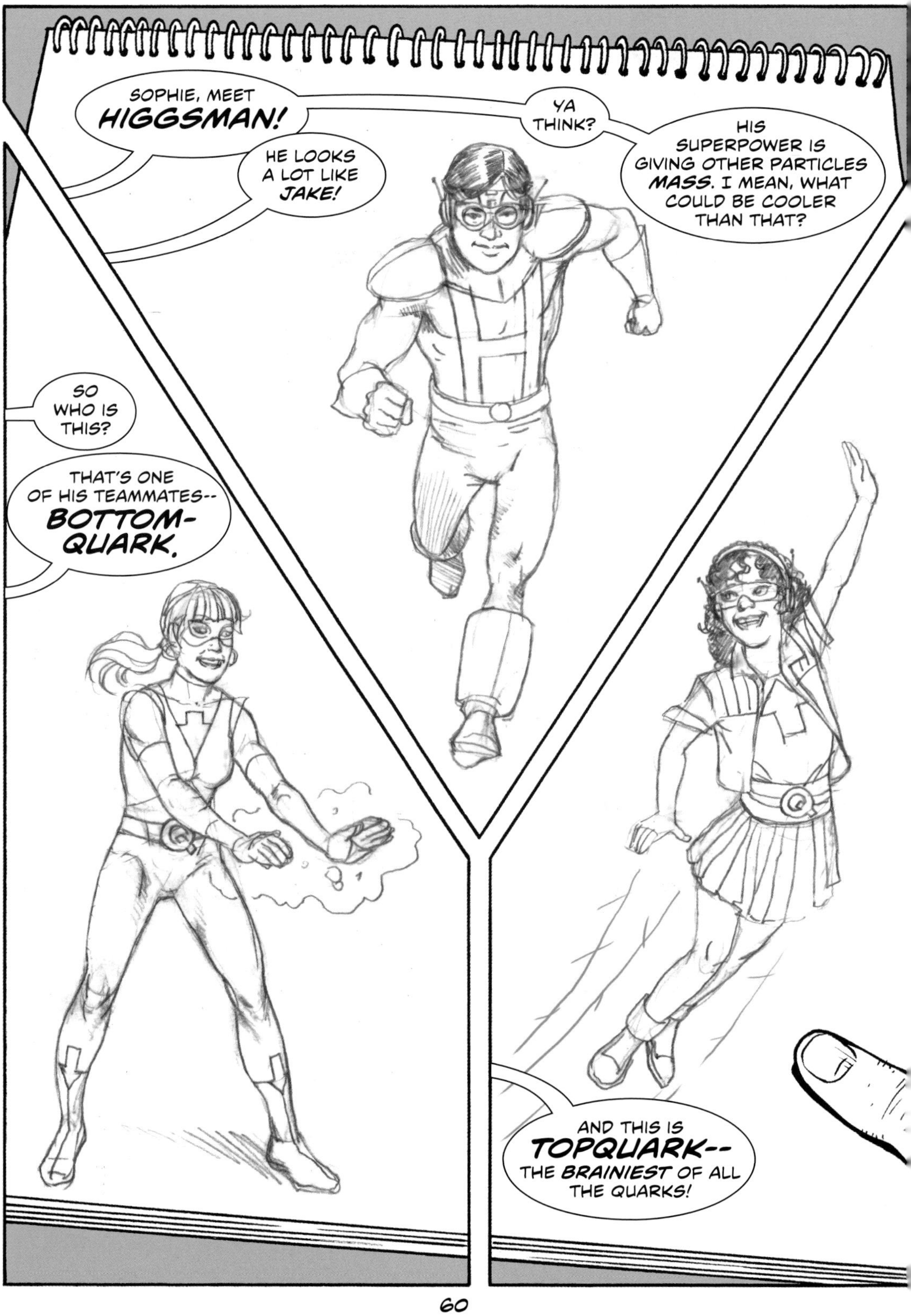
SOPHIE, MEET HIGGSMAN!
HE LOOKS A LOT LIKE JAKE!
YA THINK?
HIS SUPERPOWER IS GIVING OTHER PARTICLES MASS. I MEAN, WHAT COULD BE COOLER THAN THAT?
SO WHO IS THIS?
THAT'S ONE OF HIS TEAMMATES-- BOTTOM-QUARK.
AND THIS IS TOPQUARK-- THE BRAINIEST OF ALL THE QUARKS!

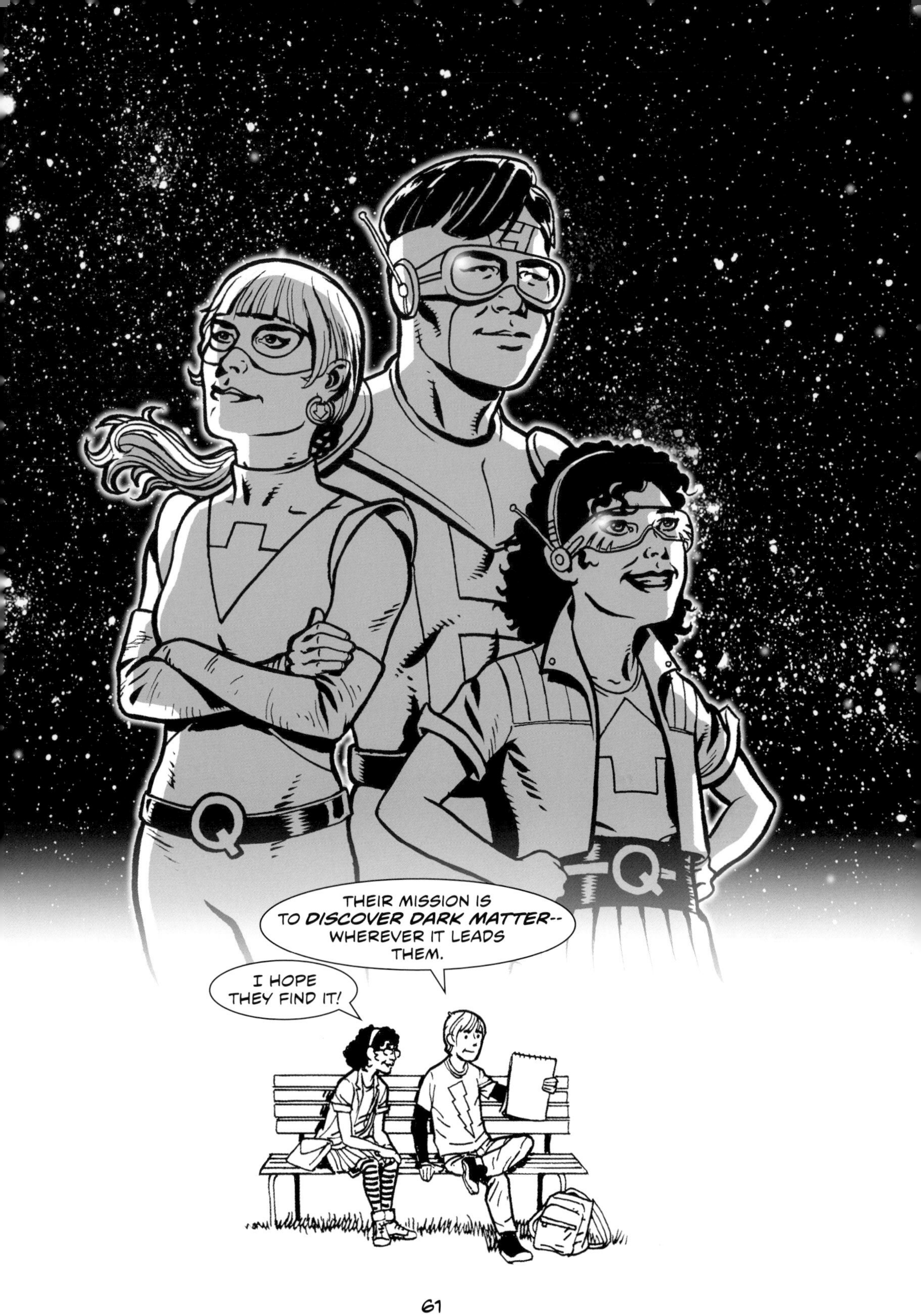
THEIR MISSION IS TO ***DISCOVER DARK MATTER***-- WHEREVER IT LEADS THEM.
I HOPE THEY FIND IT!

Unsolved Mysteries of Particle Physics

Dark matter and dark energy are among the most important unsolved mysteries in physics. But physicists will be examining other unanswered questions for years to come.

Why Is the Universe Made of Matter and Not Antimatter?

All known matter particles have corresponding antimatter particles, with the same mass but opposite electric charges. As soon as antimatter comes into contact with matter, it disappears in a flash of energy. (Scientists have learned this through making antimatter in colliders.) Since scientists theorize that the big bang should have created equal amounts of matter and antimatter, people wonder: Why didn't matter and antimatter cancel each other out at the very beginning? Somehow—no one is quite sure *how*—a tiny bit of matter gained an edge on antimatter. It's possible that matter won out because antimatter particles decay at a faster rate than matter particles. In fact, scientists are testing that hypothesis at the Large Hadron Collider!

Why Is Gravity So Weak Compared with the Other Fundamental Forces?

One theory says that gravity seems so weak relative to the other forces because people just don't feel its full force. According to this theory, part of gravity spreads to other dimensions. Humans live their everyday lives in three spatial dimensions (and in time, the fourth dimension). But additional, hidden dimensions may exist on a very small scale. Picture an acrobat walking a tightrope. The acrobat can move backward or forward, but not left, right, up, or down. But an ant walking along that tightrope can also travel *around* the rope. The ant lives on a smaller scale, and its world includes that extra dimension.

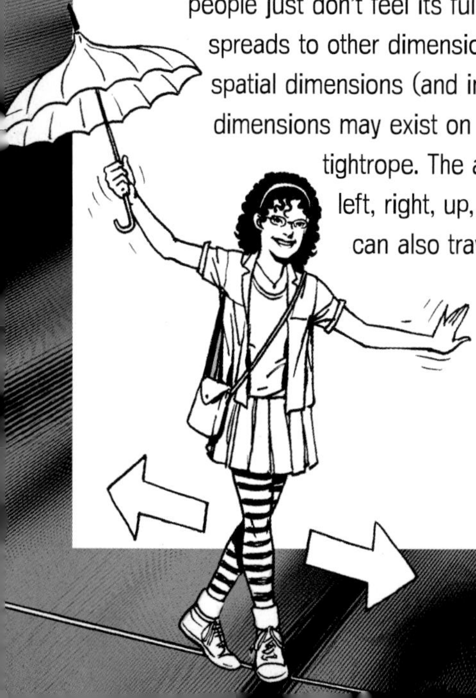

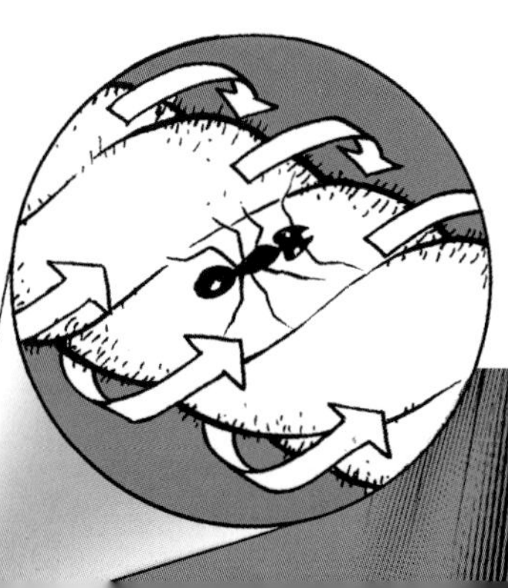

If gravity carrier particles (gravitons) exist, scientists might be able to make them at the European Organization for Nuclear Research. But the particles would immediately disappear into that extra dimension. The scientists, operating within our three-dimensional world, would only see that a piece of the puzzle was missing. However, if they were able to look at the rest of the puzzle—the other products of a collision—they would see some missing energy that might reveal more about the graviton.

Is It Worth It?

Particle physics research isn't cheap. Construction of the Large Hadron Collider required about $4.75 billion. Use of the collider requires an additional $1 billion every year. The money comes from the governments and institutions of participating countries. While many of the physicists at the LHC are simply interested in learning more about how the universe works, society often reaps the benefits of research in surprising ways.

Because physicists are always pushing the limits of science, they often have to build their own instruments. And many of the ideas that went into building these new machines—not to mention the technology itself—are useful to the rest of the world. We wouldn't have computers, X-rays, or global positioning systems without fundamental science research. Magnetic resonance imaging (MRI)—a powerful medical diagnostic tool—uses a magnetic field and radio waves to look inside the body. It uses superconducting magnets, the same kind used at the LHC. These kinds of magnets were first built for a particle accelerator in the United States. The touch screen technology in tablets and smartphones was also developed at CERN. And a computer scientist at CERN who wanted to find a way for scientists around the world to share information invented the World Wide Web. Would you say it's worth the price tag?

Science on the Move

Scientific advances can develop quickly! In fact, as this book was going to publication, new data from the LHC indicated that scientists may have detected yet another new particle. It may come to nothing, or it could be an exciting game changer that will shake our understanding of the Standard Model. By the time you read this, we'll probably know.

Peter Higgs

Transforming the Standard Model

Peter Higgs has always been something of an outsider. He was born in the northeastern corner of England in 1929, but his family moved from place to place, following his father's job as a sound engineer with the British Broadcasting Corporation. Higgs also had severe asthma—and in the days before effective drugs, this was a really big deal. As a result of his family's frequent moves and his illness, Higgs missed a lot of school. His mother often taught him at home.

At the age of twelve, Higgs enrolled in a grammar school in Bristol, England. World War II was raging during this time, and Bristol took heavy bombing. Shortly after arriving at his new school, Higgs fell into a crater in the playground—a crater left by a German bomb. Later, the Higgs family had to move after unexploded bombs were found across the road from their home. These events led Higgs to protest against the atomic bomb as a teenager. By this time, he had become interested in science, but unlike many physicists of the day, he wanted nothing to do with warfare.

Higgs's eyes would often wander during secondary school assemblies. More than once, he noticed a board listing his school's most honored alumni. One name appeared several times: Paul Dirac. Higgs did a little research on this Nobel Prize–winning alumni and found that Dirac was the father of quantum mechanics—the laws of physics that apply to subatomic particles. This kind of science, Higgs thought, could explain the way the world worked.

Higgs proceeded to study physics at a London college. After a series of failed experiments, he concluded that he was not cut out to work in a lab. He was better off using his brain to develop theories that others could test. At the age of twenty-one, Higgs gave a speech to a scientific society at the college. His theme— *How can scientists be sure that the observations they make are real?*—would be answered sixty-two years later by a $10 billion collider.

In 1960, Higgs took a position at a university in Edinburgh, Scotland. He became interested in the question of why particles gain mass. Skepticism surrounded the main theory of the time, but no one could figure out a better theory. Most people thought this field of research was a dead end. Higgs, ever the outsider, kept plugging away at it. One day in the summer of 1964, he had an "aha!" moment after reading a new research paper by a colleague. He spent the weekend walking the hills around Edinburgh and thinking. The paper he wrote afterward described a new type of field that would give particles mass via a carrier boson. It was published (after being rejected by an editor from CERN) in September 1964.

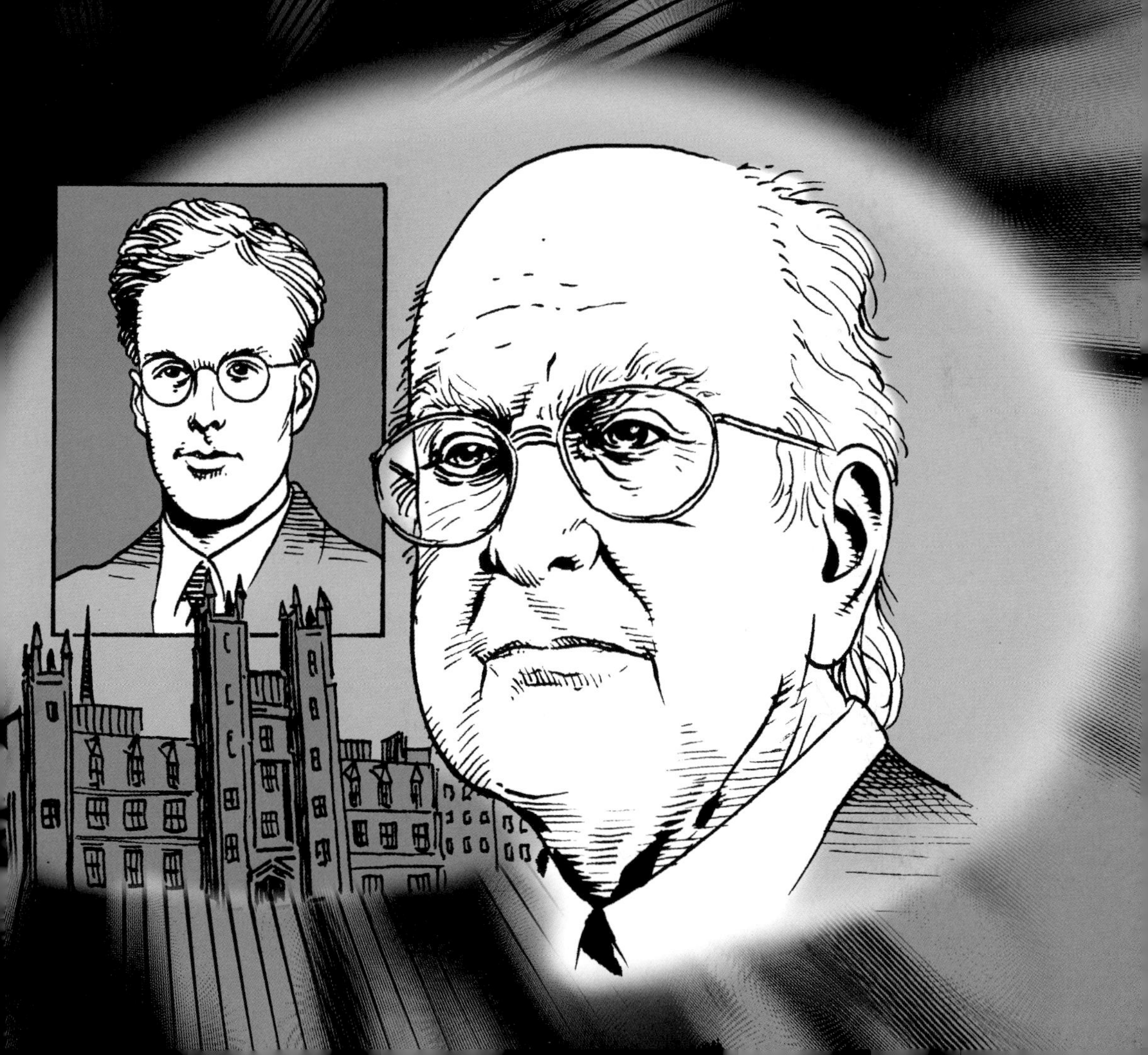

François Englert

Particle Physics Pioneer

François Englert *(top right)* was seven years old in 1940, the year the Nazis invaded his home country of Belgium. Englert and his family were forced to wear yellow Star of David patches identifying them as Jewish. As the Nazis began to send other Belgian Jews to concentration camps, François's family sent him to live with a Christian couple in a small Belgian village, while his parents and brother took refuge elsewhere. The Englerts hoped that splitting up their family might increase their chances of survival. Later, when the family reunited in another small village, a priest told village residents that the newcomers were Christian. He also baptized François so that François could attend a Catholic school.

The Englert family survived the Holocaust, although many of the Englerts' relatives did not. After the war, François developed a love for mathematics, music, and literature. However, his parents wanted him to study something practical, so like a good son, he earned a degree in electrical and mechanical engineering. His heart wasn't in it, though—Englert was more interested in learning the secrets of the universe than in building things. And so he went back to school. By 1959, he had earned his doctorate in physics.

Degree in hand, Englert accepted an offer to work for two years with Robert Brout *(top left, page 66)*, a young professor in New York. Englert returned to Belgium in 1961, but he soon missed collaborating with Brout. Brout missed working with Englert too. Brout and his wife moved to Belgium the same year.

Englert and Brout wanted to understand more about the first moments following the big bang. The two physicists proposed that immediately after this moment, particles had no mass. But as the universe expanded and cooled, a kind of phase transition took place, as when water turns to ice. An invisible field grew out of that phase transition, and any particle that interacted with that field gained mass. Englert and Brout published their findings in August 1964.

Both François Englert and Peter Higgs continued their exploration of particle physics in the decades that followed. In 2013, the Royal Swedish Academy of Sciences awarded Englert and Higgs the Nobel Prize in Physics for their theory explaining why particles have mass. Robert Brout passed away in 2011, before the discovery of the Higgs boson. Otherwise, Brout surely would have joined Englert and Higgs on the Nobel Prize stage in 2013. Three other physicists, Tom Kibble, Gerald Guralnik, and Carl Hagen *(left to right, page 66)*, published a paper describing a similar theory of particles and mass in November 1964. Although these physicists surely deserve credit for their groundbreaking work, the Royal Swedish Academy of Sciences awards the Nobel Prize to no more than three people at a time.

Glossary

accelerator: a machine that brings particles to very high speeds

annihilation: the process that occurs when a particle collides with its antiparticle, resulting in their transformation into new particles

antimatter particles: particles that are identical in all respects to their matter partners except for an opposite charge

beam: in physics, the stream of particles injected into an accelerator

big bang theory: the scientific theory that all space, time, matter, and energy originated from the violent expansion of a singular point of extremely high density and temperature

boson: a class of particles including the force-carrying particles (photons, gluons, and W and Z bosons), the Higgs boson, and the graviton

CERN: the European Organization for Nuclear Research, an accelerator laboratory near Geneva, Switzerland

collider: an accelerator in which two beams of particles make contact

dark energy: a difficult-to-detect form of energy that may accelerate the expansion of the universe

dark matter: matter that exists in the universe but that humans cannot detect because it emits no radiation that humans can observe

decay: the process in which a single particle transforms into multiple lighter particles

electromagnetic force: the physical interaction between electrically charged particles. It is one of the four fundamental forces.

electron: a lepton and, along with protons and neutrons, a building block of atoms. The electron is the least massive lepton. It carries an electric charge of -1.

event: in physics, the collision of two particles or the decay of a single particle

flavor: in physics, the term used to organize the different types of quarks and leptons

gluon: the carrier particle of the strong force

gravitational force: the force of attraction between all masses in the universe. It is the weakest of the four fundamental forces.

graviton: the theoretical carrier particle of the gravitational force

hadron: a particle made of quarks or antiquarks or both

Higgs boson: the carrier particle of the Higgs field, which is believed to give particles mass

lepton: a class of fundamental particle that does not interact strongly with other particles

LHC: the Large Hadron Collider at the CERN laboratory. The LHC is the most powerful particle accelerator in the world.

mass: the energy of a particle at rest, divided by the speed of light squared

muon: the second-heaviest lepton, with a charge of -1

neutrino: a lepton with no electrical charge and very little mass. Neutrinos participate only in weak and gravitational interactions and are very difficult to detect.

neutron: along with the proton and electron, one of the building blocks of the atom. Neutrons have no electric charge and are made of two down quarks and an up quark.

nucleus: in physics, the dense region of protons and neutrons at the center of an atom

photon: the force carrier particle of the electromagnetic force

proton: along with the neutron and the electron, one of the building blocks of the atom. Protons have a positive electric charge and are made of two up quarks and a down quark.

quark: one of the fundamental particles of matter. Quarks come in six flavors: up, down, strange, charm, bottom, and top. Only the up and down quarks are commonly found in nature.

standard model: a theory of fundamental particles and interactions

strong force: one of four fundamental forces. This force brings quarks together to make hadrons and holds protons and neutrons together in atomic nuclei.

tau lepton: the heaviest lepton, with a charge of -1

W boson: a carrier particle of the weak force

weak force: one of the four fundamental forces. It causes the decay of massive quarks and leptons into lighter particles.

Z boson: a carrier particle of the weak force

Further Information

Books

Carroll, Sean. *The Particle at the End of the Universe: How the Hunt for the Higgs Boson Leads Us to the Edge of a New World*. New York: Plume, 2013. For older readers.

Gilliland, Ben. *Rocket Science for the Rest of Us: Cutting-Edge Concepts Made Simple*. New York: DK, 2015.

Marisco, Katie. *Key Discoveries in Physical Science*. Minneapolis: Lerner Publications, 2015.

Randall, Lisa. *Higgs Discovery: The Power of Empty Space*. New York: Ecco Solo, 2013. For older readers.

Visual Media

Cosmos: A Spacetime Odyssey. First broadcast in 2014 by Fox. Directed by Brannon Braga, Ann Druyan, and Bill Pope. Written by Ann Druyan and Steven Soter. Produced by Cosmos Studios, Fuzzy Door Productions, and Santa Fe Studios, 2014. In this documentary series, scientist and host Neil deGrasse Tyson explores how humans discovered the laws of nature and found our coordinates in space and time.

Particle Fever. Directed by Mark Levinson. Produced by Mark Levinson and David Kaplan, 2013. This documentary film provides a close look at the search for—and discovery of—the Higgs boson.

Websites

ATLAS Experiment
http://www.atlas.ch

CERN: Accelerating Science
http://home.web.cern.ch

CMS (Compact Muon Solenoid) Experiment
http://cms.web.cern.ch

The Particle Adventure: Fundamentals of Matter and Force
http://www.particleadventure.org/index.html

About the Author

Sara Latta began writing about science and medicine after receiving a master's degree in immunology. Later, she earned a master of fine arts in creative writing from Lesley University in Cambridge, MA. She lives in New York City with her husband, a physicist and dean of sciences at City College of New York, and their children. Latta is a member of the Society of Children's Book Writers and Illustrators, the National Association of Science Writers, and the Authors Guild. Visit her at www.saralatta.com.

About the Illustrator

Jeff Weigel is an illustrator, author, and designer of children's books and graphic novels. Weigel illustrated the 2009 *New York Times* best seller *It's Beginning to Look a Lot Like Zombies: A Book of Zombie Christmas Carols*, and he wrote, illustrated, and designed *Stop Math*, an interactive tablet storybook. He was also a regular contributor to Image Comics' anthology title, *Big Bang Comics*, for more than 10 years. His latest book is the middle-grade graphic novel *Dragon Girl: The Secret Valley*. He has served as a graphic designer and commercial illustrator for many years as well. Find out more at www.jeffweigel.com.